THE BATTLE BEGINS

"Who gets to choose the weapons?" General Crook asked Geronimo.

"The Gunsmith was challenged," Geronimo said. "He chooses."

"Hand-to-hand," Clint said.

"The white man is afraid to fight me with a knife," the Indian warrior Chatto said, with a wicked grin. "It does not matter. I will kill him with my bare hands." Geronimo and his men formed a circle around Clint and Chatto. He and Crook also stood as part of the circle.

"Fight!" Geronimo said.

DON'T MISS THESE
ALL-ACTION WESTERN SERIES
FROM THE BERKLEY PUBLISHING GROUP

THE GUNSMITH by J. R. Roberts

Clint Adams was a legend among lawmen, outlaws, and ladies. They called him . . . the Gunsmith.

LONGARM by Tabor Evans

The popular long-running series about U.S. Deputy Marshal Long—his life, his loves, his fight for justice.

SLOCUM by Jake Logan

Today's longest-running action Western. John Slocum rides a deadly trail of hot blood and cold steel.

BUSHWHACKERS by B. J. Lanagan

An action-packed series by the creators of Longarm! The rousing adventures of the most brutal gang of cutthroats ever assembled—Quantrill's Raiders.

THE GUNSMITH

197

APACHE RAID

J. R. ROBERTS

JOVE BOOKS, NEW YORK

APACHE RAID

A Jove Book / published by arrangement with
the author

PRINTING HISTORY
Jove edition / June 1998

The Penguin Putnam Inc. World Wide Web site address is
http://www.penguinputnam.com

ISBN: 0-515-12293-9

A JOVE BOOK®
Jove Books are published by The Berkley Publishing Group,
a member of Penguin Putnam Inc.,
200 Madison Avenue, New York, New York 10016.
JOVE and the "J" design are trademarks
belonging to Jove Publications, Inc.

PRINTED IN THE UNITED STATES OF AMERICA

10 9 8 7 6 5 4 3 2 1

THE GUNSMITH

197

APACHE RAID

ONE

APRIL 1883

When Clint Adams rode into San Carlos, Arizona, he had no idea he was riding into the middle of history. He thought he was riding into a small border town at the foot of the Sierra Madre Mountains for some rest, and a beer, and some food.

He left his horse at the livery and walking to the hotel thought that he was able to feel some tension in the air. Of course, every so often—and more often than he liked—it was *his* appearance in a town that caused tension. He did not think that was the case in this instance, however.

He checked into the hotel, left his rifle and saddlebags in the room, and then repaired to the nearest saloon for a beer before finding someplace to eat.

When he entered the Broken Lance saloon he felt that tension again. Men were seated at tables with drinks, a few were lined up at the bar. Some of them were soldiers. There were a couple of girls working, but none of the men seemed interested, which Clint found odd. They were attractive enough, especially the short brunette. Not a beauty, but she drew the eyes, all right.

Clint went to the bar and the bartender gave him a wary look—wary, and weary.

"What'll ya have?"

"Beer."

"Comin' up."

The bartender came back with the beer and Clint asked him the question he had in his mind.

"What's going on?"

"Mister, you're from out of town."

"So?"

"So take my advice," the man said, "drink your beer, mount up, and keep ridin'. This ain't no place to be."

Before Clint could ask what he meant the man moved down to the other end of the bar where he stood staring sulkily into air. Clint did not want to talk to the man again, so he sipped his beer.

Usually, a lot can be learned from listening to conversations going on in a saloon. Before long you can find out who the sheriff is, who's in jail, who just go out of jail, what two men are fighting over what woman, what marriage is breaking up, who's going out of business—just about anything you'd want to know, and a lot of stuff you didn't.

This place was different because nobody was talking, at all.

"Passing through?"

Clint turned his head and looked at the woman standing next to him. It was the short brunette, and up close Clint could see that she wasn't a beauty, and yet she was sexy. It was something in the way she held her mouth, something about her attitude, the way she stood. She had a good body, too, pale, flawless skin, breasts that were probably not as big as they looked because they were pressed together by something only she knew she was wearing, but they were nice, just the same.

"I'm Ginny."

"Clint."

"Glad to meet ya," Ginny said.

"And you, too. It's kind of quiet around here, isn't it?"

She rolled her eyes and said, "Real quiet, and boring. There ain't a stiff dick in the room."

Clint kept from laughing and asked, "Not even the soldiers?"

"Them most—or least—of all."

"What's the problem?"

She cocked her head to one side and looked at him.

"You got any problem in that department?"

"Not that I know of."

"Wanna come upstairs and prove it?"

"Not if it's going to cost me anything."

"A freebee?"

He smiled and said, "Not if you don't want to. See, I just don't make a habit of paying for it."

"Well," she said, "if I got to do it on my own time it won't be until later . . . but okay. A freebee."

"What makes me so special?"

"I don't know," she said, poking him in the ribs with one ruby red nail, "I guess we're gonna find out later, ain't we? Meet me back here about eight."

"This place closes at eight?" he asked, surprised.

"No," she said, "but that's when I get off. Will you be here?"

"Sure," Clint said, "why not." Suddenly, he wanted nothing more than to see her naked—and she knew it.

"Okay," she said. "See you then."

"You won't tell me what's going on?"

"Not until later, friend," she said, and sashayed away.

Clint returned to his beer and as he was reaching the bottom of it waved the bartender over.

"Another?"

"No," Clint said. "Where can I get something to eat?"

"Café down the street serves a good steak," the man said. He was tall and thin and hardly moved his mouth when he spoke. "Out the door, go right two blocks. San Carlos Café. Can't miss it. It's got a big window."

"Okay," Clint said. "What do I owe you?"

"Forget it," the man said. "First one's on the house."

"But I didn't have a second one."

"Don't matter."

"Okay," Clint said, "thanks."

Free beer and free sex, he thought as he left the saloon. What made him so popular?

TWO

At least the bartender had been right about one thing. The café served a good steak. As a bonus, they also served good coffee.

However, the atmosphere in the place was the same as in the saloon. There were people dining together who were not talking to each other. The waitress served Clint his food with a minimum of conversation, brought him more coffee and then his bill in the same way.

Whatever was going on seemed to be affecting the whole town. He knew that he had been out of touch for some time. He'd gone off to be by himself, had not paid any attention to anyone's newspapers, or anyone's news. He wondered now what he had missed by doing that.

It wasn't only free sex he was going to get from Ginny.

Her full name was Ginny Lake, and she said she hadn't seen a stiff dick in a month of Sundays.

"Are you always so outspoken?" he asked as they reached her room.

"Yes," she said. "Does it offend you?"

"No," he said, "I like it."

She smiled and said, "That ain't all you're gonna like." She turned away from him to remove her dress and the

5

undergarment that had been pushing her breasts together and up. From what he could see, it looked like some sort of device made from whalebone, or something. He decided not to ask about it. Actually, he was too busy looking at her ass to care.

She was naked, her back to him, sliding the dress down her thighs, and when her butt came into view he knew she was right. She had a perfectly heart-shaped ass, and if nothing else matched it, it was worth coming up to her room to see it.

She rubbed her ass with the heels of her hand, kneading the flesh and then stretched, arching her back.

"Bein' on your feet all day is no fun," she said.

"I can understand that," he said. She hadn't turned around yet and he was already hard. "Are you going to turn around anytime soon?"

She looked at him coyly from over her shoulder.

"Do you want me to?"

"Very much."

"Will you pay me to?"

"No."

She shrugged and said, "Can't blame a girl for tryin'."

She turned around then, her hands on her hips. She was unabashedly naked, there was no other word for it. She was bare and reveled in it.

"I love bein' naked," she said.

"I love you being naked," he said.

Her breasts were smaller than they had appeared when she was dressed, as he had suspected, but that did not diminish their appeal one bit. They were round and firm, almost like peaches but a little larger. Her skin was pale and her nipples brown, which made them stark against their background. The tangle of bush between her legs was as black as the hair on her head, maybe even blacker.

"Now you."

"What?"

He'd been moving toward her and she put her hands out to stop him. He liked what the motion did to her breasts.

"It's your turn to undress," she said. "I want to see you."

He stopped, then stepped back and undid his gun belt first.

"Why do I get the feeling that has to be very close to the bed?" she asked.

"Yes."

"Give it here."

He gave it to her and found her standing there naked, holding his gun belt, very erotic. More and more he was impressed by her blatant sexuality.

She hung the gun on the bedpost, then turned to face him and said, "Continue."

"Do you make all your men do this?"

"Hell, no," she said, "they're usually out of their clothes before the door closes—and most of them are on me and off me before that, too. No, no, if I'm going to be giving it away tonight, Clint, I want some entertainment, also."

"Well," he said, undoing his belt, "that's always my intention when I'm with a lady."

"You must know some pretty happy ladies."

"I've never had any complaints."

"You're gonna have to prove that to me, too."

He kicked off his boots, slid his pants down around his ankles and kicked them away. The socks came next and then his shirt. The hat had already been tossed into a corner.

"Okay, okay," she said, licking her lips, "the rest."

She could already see the bulge in his shorts and knew he was hard.

"It's been too long," she said. "Let me see it."

Trying to tease her as much as she had teased him, he slowly pulled the shorts down to his ankles, bending as he did so to keep his penis out of sight. Then, abruptly,

he straightened, amazed at what he was doing, but feeling
very free and playful with this woman.

As he stood straight she saw his erection jutting upward
and caught her breath.

"Um," she finally said, "come to Mama."

THREE

As he reached for her, she pushed his hands away and said, "I'm in charge."

"Why?"

"Because I'm *not* charging."

He laughed and said, "But I've got what you want."

"Boy, do you," she said, "but you won't be disappointed. I promise."

"Oh, all right. What do you want me to do?"

"Just stand there a moment," she said, and went down on her knees.

First she ran one finger along the underside of his hard shaft. When she reached the point just below the head he jerked uncontrollably.

"That's nice," she said. "You've got the prettiest dick I've ever seen."

"Thank you."

She touched it again, this time running two fingers along the shaft down to his testicles.

"Ooh," she said, hefting them, "you're nice and tight. It's been a while for you, too, hasn't it?"

"As a matter of fact," he said, "it has."

"Mmm," she said, "I can tell by the way you're breathing, too."

She removed her hand and replaced it with her nose. She ran her nose up the length of him.

"You're so smooth," she said, "like glass. Believe me, I've seen some big, ugly ones in my time, gnarly, with lots of bulging veins, but you—you're just smooth and pretty ... and hard."

When she said "hard" she took him in her fist and began to stroke him that way. With her other hand she cupped his balls, caressing them. Clint spread his legs and moaned.

"Mmmm," she said again, "you're getting even bigger!"

Clint couldn't speak, all he could do was close his eyes and moan again. Suddenly, while his eyes were closed she engulfed him in her mouth and brought him up onto his toes.

She sucked him then slowly, moving up and down on him, wetting him, tasting him. She slid her hands around his hips to his buttocks, took hold of them tightly and began to move her head back and forth, taking all of him in, and then sliding back to the tip until he was almost out of her mouth, then taking him back in again. She did this for a few moments and then began to increase the tempo.

"Ginny," he said, tight, "remember ... it's been a while ..."

She released him just long enough to look up at him, smile, and say, "Oh, don't worry. I won't let you finish until I'm ready."

Before he could reply she took him in her mouth again and, moaning, began to suck him again.

At some other time and place Clint might have decided to show her who was in charge, but what she was doing felt so good he decided to go ahead and let her be in charge.

"Do you mind if I just enjoy this for a while?" she asked.

"Be my guest."

"Lie on the bed, then," she said. "You might as well be comfortable."

She pushed him down on the bed onto his back then got to her knees next to him and began to touch him again. She was very good at what she did, using her hands and lips to bring him almost to the point of bursting, and then stopping.

For Clint it was the sweetest kind of agony and he was anticipating the moment she would decide not to stop him—although, as time went on, he started to worry that the top of his head might come off.

But it wasn't only what she was doing to him that excited him. It was the scent she began to give off, and the way her skin felt when she brushed another part of her body against him. At one point she was bent over him, sucking him gently, and her breasts were pressed tightly to one of his thighs. Another time she slid a leg over him, and her thigh felt like silk, or velvet.

Finally, she seemed to be the one who couldn't take it anymore. Eyes shining as she straddled him, she reached between her legs for him and guided him to her portal. She was wet and he slid right in as she came down on him. She caught her breath when the entire length of him was inside of her, and then slowly began to move up and down on him. He reached for her breasts, cupped them, fondled them, popped the nipples with his thumbs. She bit her lips and moaned as he continued to touch her and she continued to ride him. She was very wet as she moved up and down on him, and the sweet, sharp smell of her seemed to fill his nostrils.

Finally, he slid his hands behind her and beneath her firm butt, feeling the wetness there. Her eyes were closed at this point, her hands pressed down on his stomach as she continued to move her butt up and down.

"Um . . . um . . . um," was all she ever said as her movements seemed to become mindless. She was seeking her own release now, and it was he who was trying to hold himself back.

At one point he slid one hand back around to the front

of her, between them, and very gently probed for her clit. When he found it she gasped and her eyes opened wide and she began to move faster on him, her breath coming in long, deep rasps.

He couldn't hold back any longer, and as she came down on him hard he felt himself explode inside of her, and thought that she was only a few seconds behind him. . . .

FOUR

The second time they went at it Clint took it upon himself to return the favor. It was Ginny's turn to lie on her back while he worked on her, teased her into a near frenzy, then backed off only to start over again.

Finally, his face was buried in her bush, his tongue working furiously. She made a high, keening sound and began to drum her heels on the bed just as furiously.

"You're gonna kill me, you're gonna kill me," she began to chant, faster and faster until it all blended together, "you'regonnakillme," and he finally took her word for it and stopped.

He mounted her then and drove himself into her again. He slid his hands beneath her, cupped her buttocks, and started to take her in long, slow, but hard strokes. She found his tempo and matched it, and then, together, they picked up speed and kept it up until the bed started to make little hops across the room. . . .

"I thought we were gonna break the bed," she said later, while she lay in the crook of his arm.

"Or the floor."

"I wonder what they thought downstairs."

"Who knows?"

"God," she said, burying her face in his shoulder.

"What?"

"I can't believe it."

"Can't believe what?"

"I can't believe what you did to me," she said. "No man has ever . . . I feel so . . . relaxed. I mean, my whole body!"

"Does this mean I held up my end of the bargain?"

"Oh, yes," she said, "definitely. This was worth a freebee."

"I'm glad to hear you're not disappointed."

"How could I be?" she asked. "Where did you learn to . . . to touch a woman like that?"

"Same place you learned to touch a man like that."

"In a whorehouse in Philadelphia?" she asked, and started laughing.

"Is that where you're from?" he asked. "Philadelphia?"

"Around there," she said.

"How did you end up here?"

"I wanted to get away from there," she said. "I figured no place was worse than that. I was wrong."

"San Carlos is bad?"

"It wasn't that bad until a few weeks ago," she said.

"Is what happened a few weeks ago the reason this town is so tense?"

"That's right."

"And now I get to hear about it?"

"Nobody told you today?"

"No one in this town is very talkative, Ginny. Why is that?"

"They're all afraid."

"Of what?"

"Indians."

Ah, the light started to dawn.

"What Indians?"

"Well, the Apaches, in general," she said. "But two in particular."

"Which two?"

"Chatto," she said, "and Geronimo."

"I thought they were on the reservation."

"You have been out of touch," she said. "They broke out some time ago, but it was only late in March that they started raiding."

"How bad?"

"They're killing a lot of people, Clint," Ginny said.

"Who's in charge of catching them?"

"General Crook."

"I met Crook once, in Washington," Clint said. "He's basically a good man. Is he here?"

"Oh, no," she said, "the soldier in charge here is Lieutenant Britton Davis."

"I've never heard of him."

"He's young, but Crook put him in charge here in San Carlos."

"Is he experienced?"

"Not very, from what I hear—and what I hear, I hear from the soldiers, who are looking for a shoulder to cry on. That's why I said I haven't seen a stiff dick in months. They're all too afraid."

"Of what?"

"Of being called out to search for Chatto and Geronimo," she said. "None of them want to go into the Sierra Madre."

"Is that where they are?"

"That's where Geronimo is," she said. "Nobody seems to know if Chatto's there, or where he is. But even knowing where Geromino is doesn't mean they'll be able to find him."

Clint nodded. At least now he understood where all the tension was coming from.

"They must have scouts."

"They do," she said. "The best."

"That means Al Sieber."

"You know him, too?"

"Enough to know that if he's around he's probably got Sam Bowman with him."

"That I don't know," she said. "I only know about Sieber because he's come to see me once or twice, when he's been in town."

"Ah," Clint said, "then I can see he hasn't lost his taste in women."

"Well, Sieber may be a good Indian scout, and he's actually not too bad in bed, but he doesn't have what you have."

"What's that?"

She reached between his legs to stroke him and said, "A pretty penis. His is all big and gnarl—"

"That's really more than I need to know about Al Sieber, thanks."

"Well," she said, ducking her head under the sheet, which muffled her voice, "maybe we shouldn't talk at all."

It took her only seconds to get him to agree.

FIVE

When Clint first rode into San Carlos he had no idea how long he was going to stay. He didn't even have any idea which way he was going to go when he left. Now that he knew about Chatto and Geronimo, he knew even less. He decided to take it one day at a time.

The next morning he woke with Ginny lying on his left arm. They'd made love twice more before falling asleep together—literally twined together, except for Clint's right arm, which he always kept free.

Now he slid the left one from beneath her without waking her and got up. He got dressed, looked around for something to use to leave a note, but found nothing. He considered waking her to say good-bye but decided against it. He'd simply stop in at the saloon and see her later.

He admired her sleeping form for a few moments, then left her room and found his way to his hotel. In his room he poured some water into a basin and used it to wash up. There had been a soldier across the street when he came in. Now he walked to the window to look outside and the soldier was gone. He decided to have breakfast in the hotel. That would make it easier for them to find him.

• • •

He was halfway through his steak and eggs when the soldier appeared. He'd wondered what rank they would send to see him, and it turned out to be a sergeant.

"Excuse me, sir?" The man presented himself at the table. Clint looked up and examined him. He was probably five or six years in the service, but the stripes on his arms looked new.

"Sergeant." Clint asked, "What can I do for you?"

"Sir, my name is Sergeant Samuel Jennings. My commanding officer, Lieutenant Britton Davis, asks that you come and see . . . him at your convenience."

"At my convenience?"

"Yes, sir . . . but sometime today."

"I see. Can you tell me what it's about, Sergeant Jennings?"

"No, sir," the man said. "That will be for him to do, sir. I've just been sent to, uh, ask you."

"To ask me."

"Yes, sir."

Clint had a feeling the sergeant would have liked to do more than ask him. Maybe, if he refused to go and see the lieutenant, the sergeant would get his chance. But then, why make things difficult?

"All right, Sergeant," Clint said, gesturing with his steak knife, "tell your commander I'll be along as soon as I finish my breakfast."

"And how long would that be, sir?"

"Oh, I don't know, Sergeant," Clint said. "This steak is kind of tough. Why don't we play it safe and say an hour?"

"An hour it is, sir," the sergeant said, and turned without another word and left.

Clint had lied. The steak wasn't tough at all and he was finished with his breakfast within fifteen minutes of the sergeant's departure, but he didn't want to jump too quickly when the army called for him. He'd had some dealings with the army in the past, some good, and some bad. He wanted this meeting to be on his terms.

So he ordered another pot of coffee.

Lieutenant Britton Davis was inexperienced. He knew that his command here in San Carlos was temporary, but he intended to make the most of it. When he heard that Clint Adams—the Gunsmith—was in town he saw an opportunity to show some initiative. Although inexperienced, he was well versed in the history of the country he loved so much. He knew much about past uprisings between the white man and the Indians, and somewhere in that history was the name "Clint Adams."

Of course, the name of the Gunsmith had appeared throughout America's history for the past twenty years and more, but the incident he had in mind had specifically to do with Indians—Quanah Parker, if his memory was correct. He just needed a little time to sort it out in his head.

The knock on the door annoyed him and he called out, "Come."

The door opened and his aide, Corporal Benson, stepped in.

"Sir, Sergeant Jennings to see you."

"All right, let him in."

Jennings stepped into the room and stood at attention in front of Davis's desk.

"At ease, Sergeant."

"Yes, sir!"

"Did you see Adams?"

"Yes, sir."

Davis waited a moment, then said, "And? Come on, Sergeant, don't make me have to drag it out of you."

"Sir, he was having breakfast at his hotel and said he would be here in an hour."

"In an hour?" Davis asked. "Not within the hour?"

"No, sir," Jennings said, "he specifically said he'd be here in an hour."

So he had an hour to search his memory for the reference he wanted.

"All right, Sergeant, very good," Davis said. "That's all. Dismissed."

"Yes, sir," Jennings said, "thank you, sir."

He came to attention again and saluted. When Davis returned the salute the sergeant left his office, closing the door behind him.

Davis stood, walked to the door, and opened it.

"Corporal, I don't want to be disturbed until Clint Adams shows up in an hour. Understood?"

"Yes, sir!"

Davis closed the door and returned to his desk. He took some deep breaths, leaned his head back, and began searching his memory.

SIX

Sergeant Jennings had left so abruptly that Clint hadn't had time to ask for directions to Lieutenant Davis's office. He obtained them from the desk clerk of the hotel, though, and presented himself to Davis's aide an hour and ten minutes after Jennings's departure.

"Corporal, my name is Clint Adams. I'm here to see the lieutenant."

"Yes, sir," the corporal said, "the lieutenant is expecting you. If you'll wait one minute I'll tell him you're here."

"Thank you."

The lieutenant's office was a two-room shack that seemed to have been hastily erected of plywood to accommodate him. It was a temporary headquarters that befitted a temporary commander.

The corporal reappeared from the other room and left the door open.

"You can go in, sir."

"Thank you."

Clint walked past the corporal into the lieutenant's "office." Lieutenant Britton Davis was standing behind his desk, a tall, sandy-haired man in his thirties.

"Mr. Adams," he said, extending his hand. "Thank you for coming so soon."

Clint shook the soldier's hand and said, "There's no telling how long I'll be in town, Lieutenant. I thought I should come as soon as possible."

"Will you have a seat?"

"Will this take long?"

"I would feel less rushed if we were sitting."

"All right, then," Clint said and sat. Davis did, as well.

"I don't know how much you've heard about our situation hereabouts, Mr. Adams."

"Just that Chatto and Geronimo are causing trouble."

"It's more than just trouble," Davis said, "it's a real concern to innocent people all along the border. From a camp in the Sierra Madre they are executing well planned raids in New Mexico and Arizona. We can't get there in time to be effective, and in any case, they either flee back into the mountains, or into Mexico."

"Where you can't go."

"Not yet," Davis said, "but we're working on that. Meanwhile I've been instructed by General Crook to keep my men on alert. As soon as I receive the order I'll be sending them to San Bernardino Springs to join up with him and many other men. From there the general will lead them into the Sierra Madre to hunt down Chatto, Geronimo, and their men."

"What size force will this be, Lieutenant?"

"In excess of two hundred men."

"And will you be going?"

Davis's eyes wavered for a moment, a sign that he was unhappy with the answer he had to give.

"I am to remain here with a skeleton force. I would, of course, like to accompany the general—"

"Of course you would," Clint said. "I'm sorry I asked."

"That's all right."

"If you don't mind me asking some more questions?"

"Please, feel free."

"How many braves do Chatto and Geronimo have?"

"We have conflicting reports," Davis said, "but we believe Chatto has about twenty-six men, while Geronimo may have as many as fifty.''

"Two hundred soldiers shouldn't have much trouble with raiding parties that small.''

"We think not,'' Davis said, "but we have to find them first.''

"I understand Crook has Al Sieber with him.''

"That's correct.''

"Then finding the Apaches shouldn't be that hard.''

"We want to make sure, Mr. Adams,'' Davis said. "That's why I would like to ask you to accompany General Crook's force into the Sierra Madre.''

"Me?'' Clint asked, surprised. "Why me?''

"Well, sir, you have a certain reputation—''

"Which reputation is that, Lieutenant?''

"Well,'' the soldier said, squirming a bit, "your reputation is varied, but I do seem to recall you had some dealings with the Comanches at one time. Quanah Parker, wasn't it?''

"That was more than ten years ago, Lieutenant.''

"Still,'' Davis said, "it does give you certain experience that a lot of our men don't have.''

"Al Sieber's not one of those men,'' Clint said. "If you've got him, you've got all the experience you need.''

"I agree,'' Davis said, "but if something were to happen to Mr. Sieber, or if he and General Crook were to, by necessity, separate—''

"Isn't Sam Bowman with Al?''

"Yes,'' Davis said, "he is . . . Mr. Adams, I sense some reluctance on your part to assist your country in this time of need.''

"Don't raise Old Glory and wave it in my face, Lieutenant,'' Clint said. "I was serving my country before you were old enough to strap on a gun.''

Davis raised both his hands in supplication and said, "Of course you were, sir. I didn't mean to imply that you weren't. It's just that—''

"Lieutenant," Clint said, "if you don't mind me saying so, I don't believe you even have the authority to ask me to do this."

Davis hesitated, then said, "Perhaps not . . ."

"Then what's the point?"

"I merely thought I might *suggest*—"

Clint stood up.

"Well, you suggested it," Clint said. "I don't think I'll act on your suggestion, though. First of all, I wouldn't want to step on General Crook's toes, or those of Al Sieber, and second, I'm not in a hurry to go up into the Sierra Madre chasing Indians. I've other, more civilian activities planned."

"But, Mr. Adams—"

"If that was all you wanted, Lieutenant?"

Davis frowned, bit his lip, then stood and said, "That was all, sir. Thank you for coming by and talking to me."

"Of course," Clint said, then left Davis's office, and the rickety structure it was in.

As soon as the door closed behind Clint Adams, Lieutenant Davis called out, "Benson!"

"Sir?"

The corporal came running in.

"Take a wire down, Corporal," he said, "and send it to General Crook in San Bernardino . . ."

SEVEN

Quanah Parker.

Clint hadn't heard that name in a long time. He had great respect for Quanah, and liked to think that the other man felt the same way. Once they had been indebted to each other, but the debt had been paid. They were never friends, and they had not seen each other again since that time.

Clint had had other dealings with Indians since then, but never as intense as the dealings he had had with Quanah on the staked plains of Texas. For Lieutenant Davis to think that he could draw on that experience and be some help against Chatto and Geronimo was ludicrous. They were different men, from very different tribes. Apaches and Comanches did not react to things the same way.

After he left Davis's office he thought about mounting up and leaving, but he'd been on the trail alone for a long time. He had been looking forward to some more hot meals prepared in hotel and café dining rooms, more beer, maybe some poker, and—now—some more of Ginny Lake. He wasn't about to let a young lieutenant's impetuousness make him change his plans.

Even though it was before noon, he decided to see if the saloon was open.

• • •

In San Bernardino, on the border between Arizona and Mexico—actually, Sonora—General George Crook read Lieutenant Britton Davis's wire, then folded it, tucked it into his blouse pocket, and called for his aide.

"Sir?" Lieutenant Will Forsythe stepped smartly into the general's tent.

"Get me Captain Crawford, on the double."

"Yes, sir."

Before the aide could leave, Crook called, "And find Al Sieber, as well."

"Sir."

Crook took the message out of his pocket and looked at it again. He had no idea how reliable Lieutenant Davis was. That was why he needed Crawford. And while he had met Clint Adams before, he needed the opinion of someone who knew him better. That was Al Sieber.

Crawford was the first to arrive, entering the tent and snapping to attention.

"You wanted to see me, sir?"

"At ease, Captain," Crook said. "I need to ask you about your second at San Carlos."

Crawford frowned as he stood at ease.

"Lieutenant Davis? Has something happened, sir?"

"It seems your second is attempting to use some initiative. Is this, uh, surprising to you?"

"Oh, no, sir," Crawford said. "Davis is a good man, sir, just a little short on seasoning. He really wants to go into the Sierra Madre, and Mexico, when we get permission."

"I'll be going into Sonora and Chihuahua soon enough to obtain that permission, Captain. For now I need to know how reliable Britton Davis is."

"I would say . . . very much so, sir."

"Yes," Crook said, "you would say so, wouldn't you?"

"Sir, may I ask what brought this question on?"

"Yes," Crook said, "you may." However, he had no

intention of answering at the moment. "You're dismissed, Captain."

Crawford, who had thought he was going to get an explanation, looked puzzled and hesitated just a moment.

"I said dismissed, Captain."

Crawford snapped to attention, said, "Yes, sir," and saluted. After Crook returned the salute, the man turned and left the tent.

Moments later Al Sieber arrived. He did not stand at attention, for Sieber was not in the service but was, rather, Chief of Scouts for Crook. The men had a very different relationship than did Crook and his officers. Sieber was younger than Crook by about ten years, and had respect for the man. Crook was generally acknowledged as the finest Indian fighter ever produced by the United States Army, and yet when he first came to the San Carlos Reservation he knew he had a lot to learn about the Apaches, and he learned most of it from Sieber.

"You wanted me, General?"

"Al," Crook said, "you know Clint Adams, don't you?"

"Yes, sir," Sieber said, "some."

"Better than I do, I'll warrant," Crook said. "I met the man once in Washington, D.C."

"What did you think of him then, sir?"

"I thought he was . . . somewhat irreverent."

Sieber smiled and said, "That's what he was when I met him."

"How long have you known him?"

Sieber rubbed his jaw and said, "Must be goin' on twelve years, though I ain't seen him more'n twelve times, all told."

"Still," Crook said, "you know him."

"Yes, sir," Sieber said. "I do. What's this all about, General?"

"I just got a wire from Lieutenant Britton Davis. Seems Adams is in San Carlos."

"He is, huh?"

"Al, how would you like to have him with us when we go after Geronimo and Chatto?"

"I'd dearly love it, sir," Sieber said, speaking frankly. "He's worth any five of these boys in blue you got with you, I'll tell you that."

Crook stiffened.

"My men are good men, Sieber!"

"Don't go gettin' yourself all riled up, General," Sieber said. "All I said was, they ain't none of them the Gunsmith. That man can shoot prettier than anyone I ever seen."

"We can certainly use that," Crook said. "Does he have any experience with Indians?"

"Comanches, and some others."

"Comanches?"

"Yes, sir," Sieber said, "Quanah Parker."

Crook's eyes lit up.

"Ah," he said, "that's impressive . . . but can he take orders?"

Sieber laughed and said, "No, sir. If you think I'm a tough nut to order around, wait until you try it with him."

"Will it be worth my time to take steps to get him?" Crook asked. "Apparently, he's reluctant to come along."

"I'd say it'd be worth however much time you gotta spend, General."

"All right, then," Crook said. "You'd better get started. It's a hundred and thirty miles back to San Carlos."

"Started?"

"That's right," Crook said. "You're going back there to talk to the man."

"I don't know that I could convince him, sir."

"I don't need you to convince him, Sieber," Crook said, "just talk to him and keep him occupied. Don't let him leave San Carlos until you hear from me. Do you hear, Al?"

"I hear you, General," Sieber said. "You know, you got Sam Bowman there—"

"You'll be bringing Bowman back with you," Crook said, "as well as the rest of the scouts and most of the men."

"You figurin' on having your permission to enter Mexico before long?"

"I'll be going into Sonora and Chihuahua any day now," Crook said, "and if I have my way—and I believe I will—we'll be moving out come May first."

"Guess I better get to ridin', then," Sieber said. "Sure didn't think I'd be gettin' ordered to baby-sit an old friend."

"Luckily," Crook said, "there are times when you *do* follow orders, Mr. Sieber."

"Yes, sir," Sieber said, "when it suits me. I think this could be real interestin'—*real* interestin'."

"Well, Mr. Sieber," Crook said, "I guess my lot in life is to keep *your* life interesting."

"Sir—"

"You'd better get moving."

"Yes, sir. I'm on my way. There's still plenty of light."

"Take the best horse we've got," Crook said, "and don't stop until you get there."

"Begging the general's pardon," Sieber said, "but I own the best horse we got, and I wouldn't be takin' no other."

"You're impudent, at best, Mr. Sieber."

"You ain't seen nothin' yet, sir."

EIGHT

Clint was sitting in the saloon when he saw Sam Bowman come walking in. The man hadn't changed much, probably just gotten older like everyone else. He was tall, broad-shouldered, shaggy and bearded. He went straight to the bar and ordered a beer.

Clint was surprised to see Bowman. When he'd asked the lieutenant if Sieber had Bowman with him the man's answer had been yes, yet here he was.

"You know him?"

He turned his head and saw Ginny standing next to him. He'd felt her sidle up to him.

"Sam Bowman."

"That's right. You know a lot of people, I guess."

"Some," Clint said. "You know how long he's been in San Carlos, Ginny?"

"Not exactly," she said. "He's probably been in and out for the better part of six months, though."

"How about this time?"

She shrugged.

"Can't tell ya, Clint. Sorry."

He looked at her and said, "That's okay, Ginny. You look real nice tonight."

She was wearing a dress much like the one she'd worn

31

last night, but that one was green and this one was red. Again, her breasts were pushed up and together to give her more cleavage.

"You look radiant, in fact," he said.

"Thank you, sir." She put her hand on his shoulder. "Are you and Bowman friends?"

"Acquaintances," Clint said. "In fact, I don't even know if he'll remember me."

At that moment Bowman turned, beer in hand, glanced in Clint's direction and looked surprised.

"Well, I'll be—" he said, and came striding over to where Clint was seated.

"I guess he remembers you," Ginny said. "I'll leave you two alone. See you later?"

"Definitely."

As she left, Bowman said aloud, "Clint Adams, by my soul."

"Sam," Clint said, standing.

Bowman put his hand out and mangled Clint's in an iron grip.

"What are ya doin' here?" Bowman asked.

"Just passing through, Sam. Have a seat."

They both sat and Bowman stared across the table at him.

"Why would you be ridin' through this area?" he asked. "Don't you know what's goin' on?"

"I've been hearing something about Chatto and Geronimo and some rogue Apaches who broke from the reservation."

"Crook is determined to get them back, Clint, one way or another. That's why he's got me and Al and some others. You know Al Sieber, right?"

"Real well," Clint said.

"Sure, you do," Bowman said, "what am I thinkin'? You two are friends."

"How is Al?"

"He's just fine," Bowman said. "He's camped along the San Bernardino River right now with the general."

"I hear you and some men will be heading out that way soon."

"Soon as we get the word. Say, why don't I get you a colder beer? We got some catchin' up ta do."

"Okay, fine."

"Be right back."

Bowman went to the bar and returned with a fresh beer, setting it down gently in front of Clint so as not to spill the foam head over the sides. Clint remembered Bowman as a man with steady nerves—the steadiest he'd ever seen.

They talked first of how long it had been since they had seen each other, and when that was established they talked a bit about what they had been doing since then. Bowman had generally been doing the same thing, scouting for the army, sometimes with Sieber and sometimes without him.

"Crook wanted both of us for this thing, though," Bowman said.

"My guess would be," Clint said, "that he's going to use one of you to find Chatto and the other to find Geronimo."

"Maybe," Bowman said. "Do you know Crook?"

"Met him once," Clint said, "in Washington, D.C. We didn't get along."

"Oh? Why not?"

"He likes to give orders," Clint said, "even at Washington parties."

"Yeah, that's our Crook," Bowman said, "but he's the best damned Indian fighter I've ever seen."

"I don't doubt it."

"And you know why?"

"Why?"

"He knows when to ask questions," Bowman said, "and he knows when to delegate authority."

"He's a smart man, most of the time," Clint said, "I'll give him that."

"He's so smart," Bowman said, "you'd better not let him know you're here."

"Why not?"

"Because he'll try to recruit you, that's why."

"Already been tried."

"By who?"

"Fella named Britton Davis."

"The pup," Bowman said, nodding. "Yeah, he'd try to do that to impress Crook."

"Well, it didn't work," Clint said, "so I don't know how impressed Crook will be."

"I'll tell you one thing."

"What?"

"I wouldn't mind havin' you out there with me, watching my back."

"I'll take that as a compliment, Sam."

"I mean it as one," Bowman said. He drained his beer and pushed the empty mug away. "Well, I gotta get going. It's good to see you."

"You, too, Sam. Give Al my best when you see him."

They stood and shook hands.

"How long you plan on bein' in town?" Bowman asked.

"A day or two, no more," Clint said.

"Don't blame you," Bowman said. "Get this place behind you, Clint. Get away from the border, in fact."

"I'll take that as good advice."

Bowman nodded and said, "Meant it as good advice. Be seein' ya."

Bowman went out the door and Clint sat back down. It hadn't dawned on him that maybe the young officer had been trying to impress his commander. Well, sorry, Lieutenant Davis, but it just isn't going to happen, Clint thought, not at my expense.

NINE

Britton Davis examined the message in his hand again. It had arrived soon after he'd sent his own, early that afternoon. He'd had it on his desk since then. Crook had advised him to make sure Clint Adams didn't leave town until Al Sieber got there. Davis knew what that meant. Sieber was going to talk Adams into joining Crook's force, and then the scout would get the credit.

His aide knocked on the door, opened it, and said, "Sam Bowman, sir."

"Send him in."

Bowman came in, holding his hat in his hand and mangling it.

"Well, Mr. Bowman? Did you see Clint Adams?"

"Yes, sir, I did."

"And?"

"He don't seem in a hurry to leave, sir." Bowman didn't dare tell the lieutenant that he had advised Clint to leave town.

"Good, good," Davis said. "That's what Crook wants."

"When will Al Sieber be arriving, sir?"

"I guess that depends on whether or not he stops riding when it gets dark."

"Not if the general wants him to get here as soon as he

can,'' Bowman said. "Al will ride all night."

"If he does that," Davis said, "he'll be here by tomorrow. We just have to make sure Adams doesn't leave until then."

"Beggin' your pardon, sir," Bowman said, "but if Clint Adams decides to leave town there ain't nobody gonna be able to stop him."

"The United States Army will stop him, Mr. Bowman," Davis said. "I can assure you of that."

"The army can try, sir."

"The army never tries, Mr. Bowman," Davis said stiffly, "the army *does*!"

"Yes, sir. Well, if that's all you'll be needin' me for—"

"I'd like you to keep an eye on Adams."

"Can't do that, Lieutenant," Bowman said with a shake of his head.

"I can make it an order—"

"All I'm sayin', Lieutenant," Bowman added, "is that it wouldn't be wise to have me watch him. He knows me, and he'll spot me. If that happens he'll know something's afoot."

"Hmm," Davis said reluctantly, "you have a point."

"My advice would be to have a man watch his hotel, and another watch the livery. If the man at the hotel misses him, the man at the livery won't. He won't be able to leave without his horse—and he *wouldn't* leave without that horse."

"You're quite right, Mr. Bowman," Davis said. "I believe I've heard the stories about the Gunsmith and his famous black gelding . . ."

"Duke."

"That's right," Davis said, "Duke. All right, Mr. Bowman. You can go."

"Yes, sir," Bowman said. "Sir?"

"Yes?"

"Any idea when we'll be joining General Crook?"

"Any day now," Davis said, "any day."

"That's good," Bowman said. "The waitin' is drivin' me crazy."

Davis stared at Sam Bowman and saw a man who looked as calm as a man could be.

"Yes," he said, "I can see that, Mr. Bowman. Dismissed."

"Yes, sir."

"Don't close the door."

"Yes, sir."

As Bowman went out, Davis shouted, "Benson!"

"Yes, sir," the aide said, appearing in the door.

"Get me our best horse handler."

"Uh, who would that be, sir?"

"I don't know, Corporal," Davis said. "Find out who it is, and get him here."

"Yes, sir."

Davis couldn't wait for the day when he'd be a general and have a lieutenant for an aide.

A lowly lieutenant.

TEN

Clint spent the night with Ginny again, and the beginning was spent quite pleasantly. They did whatever they hadn't done the night before, and afterward—damp and exhausted—they lay together in his bed and talked.

Clint told her about his conversation with Sam Bowman, about Geronimo and Chatto, and General Crook. He also told her about Al Sieber.

"You know all these people?" she asked.

"I know Al Sieber," he said. "I've met Crook and am acquainted with Bowman."

"What about Geronimo and Chatto?"

"I've never had the pleasure of meeting either gentleman," he said.

"Gentleman?"

"Well," he said, "not knowing them, who am I to assume they are anything but?"

"Excuse me?" she said. "Don't they kill people?"

"So I've been told."

"For no good reason?"

"If there's one thing I've learned over the years," he said, "it's that there's usually a reason when one person kills another."

"For a savage?"

39

"Who's to say who is savage?"

"Well, I've heard stories . . ." she said.

"I'm sure you've heard stories about me, too, haven't you?"

"Well, yes . . ."

"And do you believe them all?"

"Well . . . not now that I've met you . . ."

"Why not give Geronimo the same courtesy?" he asked. "Reserve your opinion until you've met him."

"I'm *not* gonna meet him," she said with great finality. "I don't want to meet him."

"Well," he said, "to tell you the truth, neither do I."

"So you're not going to go?"

"No, I'm not."

She snuggled closer to him and said, "Good, 'cause I'm not ready for you to get killed. I'm not done with you yet."

"You're not?"

"No."

"What did you have in mind?"

"Well, maybe this . . ."

"Oh."

"Or maybe just this . . ."

"Oh . . . well . . ."

"Or how about . . . this?"

"Yeah," he said, "that would do it . . ."

ELEVEN

Ginny left at first light, and Clint left his room soon after that. He went down and had breakfast in the hotel and noticed among the diners a few soldiers. There were two sitting together, and one surly-looking man seated alone. They were all the same rank, private. He wondered if any of these men had been sent to keep an eye on him. Would a private be sent, or someone of a higher rank?

For a moment it occurred to Clint to take the advice of the bartender and leave town. Would that be running away? And if so, from what? All the lieutenant had done was request that he help the army out with a little problem, and he had refused. He had the right to refuse, didn't he? He wasn't about to be drafted into service.

He ordered his breakfast and asked the waiter if he had a newspaper.

"A local one?" the man asked.

"Anything."

Clint knew that people left newspapers behind in restaurants and hotels all the time. He didn't care where it was from, he just wanted something to read while he was eating.

The waiter returned with his coffee and a copy of *The El Paso Gazette*.

"Is this good enough?"

Clint noticed that the paper was a week old.

"It will do," he said. "Thank you."

El Paso was close enough to the action that there were some pieces written about the "situation." One was about Crook, the Great Indian Fighter, and another about Geronimo, the Savage. Slightly slanted, to say the least.

Clint knew that the white man had a habit of signing treaties that they had no intentions of honoring. He also knew that some of the Indians—like Geronimo—did not stand for this. Others did. It was Clint's theory that the army thought that the occasional "renegade" was a small price to pay for keeping the other Indians in line and on the reservation. They believed that once an Indian was on the reservation, nine times out of ten he was there to stay. Clint had once heard an army officer—could it have been Crook, at that Washington party?—opine that Indians were inherently lazy, and that they breathed a sigh of relief when they were finally consigned to a reservation.

Not so Geronimo, or Chatto, apparently.

When his breakfast came he folded the newspaper and put it down on the other side of the table. He gave his full attention at that point to his steak and eggs, and stopped worrying about Indians, or about soldiers who might or might not be watching him.

Across the street Corporal Evan Watkins wondered how he had come to be chosen for this job. He knew all about Clint Adams—the Gunsmith—and the last thing he wanted was for Adams to find out that he was watching him. He wondered if Adams would understand that he had been ordered to do this and that it was nothing personal. He just had to keep an eye on the civilian until Al Sieber, the scout, showed up later that day. Sieber was going to have to do some heavy riding to make it, but Watkins had seen Sieber's horse. It was an Indian pony that had a lot of stamina—stamina which Sieber was going to be putting to good use.

Watkins went over the instructions he'd gotten from Lieutenant Davis that morning:

"Keep an eye on Adams, don't let him out of your sight, and above all, don't let him leave town."

The corporal wiped the sweat from his brow with his sleeve. If the Gunsmith suddenly decided to leave town, how was he supposed to stop him? Shoot him? He was more likely to get shot.

Huddled in his doorway he knew he was just going to have to hope that Clint Adams had no intentions of leaving town.

Not today.

TWELVE

When Clint left the hotel he noticed the soldier standing in a doorway across the street. He was a nervous-looking corporal. That was more like it. He decided to take a turn around town and see if the man stayed with him. Sure enough, a half an hour later the soldier was still there. More than likely he was simply keeping an eye on him. He wondered what the man would do if he went to the livery, saddled Duke, and rode out of town.

Then again, why make the man's job harder? Clint decided to go right to the source, and led the soldier to Lieutenant Britton Davis's office.

"Sir?" the lieutenant's aide said as Clint walked in.

"I'd like to see Lieutenant Davis."

"I'll . . . see if he's in, sir."

"Is there another way into his office?"

"Sir?"

"A back door?"

"No, sir."

"Then unless he went out a window," Clint said, "I'd say he was in there, right?"

"Uh . . ."

"Why don't you just tell him I'm here?"

"Yes, sir," the corporal said, "I'll do that."

45

He went into the lieutenant's office after knocking, closing the door behind him, and reappeared moments later.

"The lieutenant will see you, Mr. Adams."

"Thank you."

Clint went past the man into the lieutenant's office. Davis was standing behind his desk, his hands clasped behind his back.

"Ah, Mr. Adams," Davis said. "You've thought over what we talked about?"

"Yes, I did."

"And you've decided to join us?"

"No, I haven't."

Davis frowned.

"Lieutenant," Clint said, "you're going to have to earn your captaincy another way."

"Sir?"

"I intend to stand by my original decision," Clint said.

"That's too bad," Davis said. "A man like you would be very valuable—"

"Let's dispense with that bull, Lieutenant," Clint said. "And I'd also like you to dispense with my tail."

"Your . . . tail? I'm afraid I don't—"

"The young corporal who's been following me all morning, and watching my hotel," Clint said. "Give him a break and reassign him."

"He's, uh, only keeping an eye on you, Mr. Adams," Davis said.

"For what reason?"

"To, uh, keep you out of trouble."

"I can keep myself out of trouble, thank you."

"Still," Davis said, "a man with your reputation can't be too careful—"

"You're right about that, Lieutenant," Clint said. "I'm always careful. That's why I don't like having anyone I don't know behind me. You should remove your young man before he gets hurt."

Davis frowned again.

"Sir, are you threatening me? Or my corporal?"

"I'm just telling you," Clint said, "that a man in my position can't be too careful. Sometimes, when there's somebody behind me, I get edgy. I may not mean to, but somebody might get hurt."

"Mr. Adams—"

"Lieutenant," Clint said, "I'm leaving now. I'm going to send your corporal in to see you. Do us both—no, do all three of us—a favor and reassign him, eh?"

Clint didn't wait for a reply. He turned, went out through the outer office, and out the front door. He marched right across the street and confronted the nervous-looking corporal, who appeared ready to bolt and run.

"Soldier," Clint said, "your lieutenant would like a word with you."

"S-sir?" the man asked. "D-do you mean me?"

"I do, son," Clint said. He clapped the young man on the shoulder. He couldn't have been more than twenty-four. "I think you're about to be reassigned."

The look on the face of the young man was the same as the look on the face of a condemned man who has received a reprieve.

"Yeah, I don't blame you," Clint said, "I'd be relieved, too."

With that he walked away, hoping that the lieutenant would make the right decision for all of them.

THIRTEEN

When Al Sieber entered the saloon Clint wasn't surprised. He had already guessed that it would be Sieber they'd send to talk to him. First they'd sent Bowman to check him out, and then the young corporal to keep an eye on him. Next, if they were going to send someone to try to talk him into helping, it would have to be Al Sieber—or General Crook himself. To their credit they'd decided on Sieber rather than Crook.

Clint turned to the bartender and said, "A beer for my friend."

The bartender looked around and asked, "What friend?"

"That one," Clint said, pointing to Sieber, who was approaching the bar.

As Sieber reached him, the bartender put the beer on the bar. Clint picked it up and handed it to the scout, who accepted it with his left hand and extended his right for a handshake.

"I need this," Sieber said, taking a grateful swallow. "I've been riding hard for too long."

"How's your horse?"

"Holding up better than I am."

"You want to sit?" Clint asked. "Or make your plea standing?"

"I'll sit," said the weary-looking Sieber. "Lead the way."

Clint led the man to a back table and sat with his back to the wall.

"Still careful," Sieber said.

"Still alive," Clint said.

Sieber sat across from him, secure in the knowledge that Clint would watch his back.

"It's been a while, Clint."

"Yeah, it has. Saw Bowman yesterday morning."

"I haven't seen him yet."

"They sent him to check me out, I guess," Clint said, "see if I was going to stay."

"Why did you stay?" Sieber asked. "You must have known they'd send someone."

"I figured it would be you," Clint said. "Thought I'd stay around and say hello."

"You understand what's going on, don't you?"

"I've been told."

"Then you know why I'm here."

"You rode straight through?"

Sieber nodded.

"From San Bernardino?"

Sieber nodded again.

"Well," Clint said, "after all that I guess I owe it to you to listen."

Sieber talked for a long time, about honor, and duty, about Geronimo and Chatto and Crook, the U.S. Army, the Indians on the reservation who were being done a disservice by the renegades.

"Al, Al," Clint said, shaking his head.

"I had you up to there, didn't I?"

"You had my attention," Clint said, "but that stuff about the good of the Indians on the reservation . . ."

"Okay, okay," Sieber said, "I pushed too hard. I guess I'm more tired than I thought. I need something to eat. You want another beer?"

"Sure."

"Some food?"

"Why not?"

Sieber nodded.

"Let the army buy you some food, Clint."

"It'll take more than that, Al," Clint said.

"I know," Sieber said, "but it's a start. You mind eating here? I can get some sandwiches."

"That's fine," Clint said, "just bring the other beer while we're waiting."

"Of course," Sieber said. He stood up and Clint could see the fatigue in the way he stood. "I just hope I can stay awake."

FOURTEEN

Over sandwiches—Clint wasn't sure what they were made from, and he didn't ask—and some hard-boiled eggs—at least he knew where those came from—they caught up on old times, and had a couple more beers.

"Can we get back to the reason I'm here?" Sieber asked after a while. "I've really got to get some sleep."

"Maybe we could continue this in the morning, Al," Clint said. "I think it will take you more than one evening to talk me into the Sierre Madre."

"I'll just get a running start," Sieber said.

"Okay," Clint said, sitting back, "go ahead."

"Crook knows what he's doing, Clint," Sieber said, "and he's got me and Bowman and some other experienced men, but I have to tell you, I don't relish going into those mountains with the recruits he's got."

"Aren't they army-trained men?" Clint asked.

"Oh, sure," Sieber said, "some of them even remember all the training because it wasn't long ago that they got it. I'm tellin' you, Clint, a lot of them are kids, and some of them that ain't kids still don't know what they're in for."

"Uh-huh."

"We need experienced men."

"I'm not experienced with Indians, Al."

"Yes, you are. There was Quanah—"

"Comanches," Clint said, "not Apaches."

"It's still experience," Sieber said, "more than a lot of these boys have."

Clint sat and stared silently at Sieber.

"How am I doin'?" Sieber asked.

"It's asking a lot, Al," Clint said. "This is army business, and I'm a civilian."

"So am I."

"You're an army scout."

"I'm not in the army."

"You might as well be."

"Okay, okay," Sieber said, "so it's going to take more than one night." He drained the last of his beer and stood up. "I'm turning in. We'll continue in the morning. You will be here in the morning, won't you?"

"I'll be here," Clint said.

Sieber nodded, turned to leave, and then turned back.

"I don't want to get killed out there, Clint," he said, "and up to now, that's what I was expectin' to happen."

Sieber turned and walked out.

"You're a son of a bitch, Sieber," Clint said to his retreating back.

Clint stayed in the saloon and tried to decide between beer and poker. There was a game going, so he decided on poker. That meant no beer, because he didn't drink when he played.

For part of the game Ginny stood beside him, her hand possessively on his shoulder. He had introduced himself upon sitting down to the game, but the other four men already knew who he was.

"So I hear you're goin' into the Sierra Madre after Geronimo," one of them said to him.

"Where did you hear that?" Clint asked.

"I don't know . . . around."

"Well, you heard wrong."

"Wasn't that the scout, Al Sieber, you were talkin' to?" another man asked.

"It was," Clint said. "We're old friends."

"So he wasn't tryin' to talk you into going into the mountains with Crook?"

"He was."

"And he didn't succeed?"

Clint smiled and said, "Not yet. I raise."

"Huh?"

"You bet ten, mister," Clint said, "and I raise twenty. You don't start paying attention you're going to lose your shirt."

From there on out the other four men kept quiet and played poker.

They lost their shirts, anyway.

FIFTEEN

Once again it was Ginny Clint talked to as they tumbled into his bed that night. First, however, there was no talking. . . .

Clint ran his hands over Ginny's back, admiring the curve of her spine, the line of it as it flowed into her fine, firm buttocks. She was on her stomach, her breasts flattened beneath her, her buttocks in the air. He was on his knees behind her, his erection buried deep inside of her.

He ran his hands over her back, squeezed her buttocks, held her hips as he drove into her. With each thrust of his hips she reared back at him, matching his movements, grunting each time he drove into her, urging him on, imploring him to keep going and not stop until finally he exploded inside of her and she screamed, the sound of it muffled because her face was buried in the mattress. . . .

"You're gonna go, aren't you?"
   "I haven't decided."
   "Why don't you just leave town?"
   "I can't do that."
   "Why not?"
   "It would be too much like running away."

"So? Why can't you run away?"

"It's too hard to explain, Ginny."

"Hmph," she said, "it's a man thing, isn't it?"

He thought a moment, then said, "That's a good way of putting it, I guess."

"More men have died for that reason."

"Maybe so . . . and maybe I can keep some more from dying."

"By dying yourself?"

"That wouldn't be my first choice."

"If you go into those mountains," she said, "after Geronimo, you might not have a choice."

"Well," he replied, "like I said, I haven't decided yet."

"You'll make your friend Sieber do some more talking tomorrow, but in the end you'll give in."

"How do you know so much?"

"I've seen it before," she said.

"Seen what?"

"Men doing crazy things in the name of friendship."

"Well," he said, "like you said before, I guess it's a man thing."

SIXTEEN

"Why didn't you come to see me yesterday, when you first arrived?" Lieutenant Britton Davis demanded of Al Sieber.

"Lieutenant," Sieber said, "my assignment from General Crook was to get here and talk to Clint Adams. I did that last night, and then I got some sleep. I'm only stoppin' in here now to see you out of courtesy."

The two men stared at each other across the lieutenant's desk. They didn't like each other, that was no secret. Davis could feel Sieber's lack of respect for him, and it always made him livid. The scout was not even an army man, simply a civilian working for the army.

"Well, what did he say?" Davis asked.

"He said the same thing to me he said to you," Sieber answered, "no."

"But what can we—"

"I'm not finished talking to him," Sieber said, interrupting the younger man. "I'll get him to agree."

"How can you be sure?"

"Because Clint Adams does for his friends, Lieutenant," Sieber said. "He always has and he always will."

"And you'll use that against him?"

"I hate like hell to do it," Sieber said, "but if that's

59

what it'll take to get him to come along, then yes, I will.''

"Well . . . let me know what happens . . . will you?" He added the last two words reluctantly.

Sieber stood up and said, "I'll keep you informed, Lieutenant . . . as a courtesy."

"Yes," Davis said, "of course."

"Oh, one more thing," Sieber said.

"Yes?"

"You don't have anybody watching Adams, do you?"

"Why, no . . . why?" Davis asked. He didn't bother telling the scout that if he had asked that question yesterday the answer would have been quite different.

"Oh, Adams just wouldn't react well to that kind of pressure, Lieutenant," Sieber said. "Glad to see you figured that out."

"Yes," Davis said, "of course."

He was seething as the scout left his office.

Sieber went to Clint's hotel after stopping at the telegraph office first. He picked up something there he hoped he wouldn't have to use.

He thought about interrupting Clint's breakfast but then decided against it. Instead he figured to wait outside for Clint to put in an appearance. He was refreshed from a night's sleep and wasn't feeling rushed. He figured to have Clint wrapped up by the end of the day, and there was plenty of time for them to get to San Bernardino to join up with Crook before he made his move into the Sierra Madre.

Clint looked out his window and saw Sieber standing across the street.

"What is it?" Ginny asked.

She had not left his room early this time, as she had done on other days.

He turned and looked at her. She was covered by the bedsheet, but it clung to her every curve. He was dressed, but suddenly he felt like getting undressed and joining her in the warm bed again.

"Sieber's across the street."

"Think he's gonna try talking to you again today?" she asked.

"I know he will," Clint said. "I only hope he waits until after I've had my breakfast—speaking of which . . ."

She flopped onto her back, the sheet still covering her.

"You go ahead," she said. "I never eat breakfast. I can't even think about food until afternoon."

"Will you be working today?"

"Nope," she said, "today's my day off."

Which explained why she was still there.

"If you don't mind," she went on, "I'll just stay here for a while."

"I don't mind," he said. He walked to the bed and kissed her. She didn't open her eyes. "I'll see you later."

"Mmmm," she said, and he thought that she was asleep before he got out into the hall.

Clint had his usual breakfast and took his time eating it. Might as well let Sieber wait awhile for him outside. When he was finally done he walked through the lobby and stopped just inside the door. He was able to see outside and Sieber was still there, looking cool and patient.

Clint shook his head. If there was one thing he remembered about Al Sieber, it was that patience—which came in handy when you were dealing with Indians. Waiting for Clint to finish his leisurely breakfast had been no hardship at all for the man.

Clint decided to get it over with and stepped outside.

SEVENTEEN

When Sieber saw Clint he crossed the street immediately.

"Okay," Clint said, "you got me."

"What?" Sieber looked surprised. "What do you mean?"

"I mean I'll help you," Clint said. "I'll try to keep you alive while you look for Geronimo. That's what you wanted, isn't it?"

"Well . . . yeah . . ."

"And Crook? What's he want?"

"I guess you're gonna have to ask him that."

"When does Crook figure to make his move?"

"The beginning of May, hopefully. He has to get permission to cross the border."

"Will he get it?"

"He says yes," Sieber replied. "The Mexicans are as worried about Geronimo and his people as we are."

"All right, then," Clint said. "What do we do first?"

"We go to San Bernardino."

"And Lieutenant Davis?"

"Not him," Sieber said. "He's staying here."

"And Bowman?"

"He'll be with us," Sieber said. "We'll be taking quite

a few men away from here with us, leaving mostly a skeleton crew behind.''

"It doesn't seem as if this town would be in danger," Clint said.

"That's what we're thinking," Sieber said. "Besides, once we start chasing them they're more likely to be in front of us than behind us."

"Will we be going after Geronimo," Clint asked, "or Chatto?"

"I get Geronimo," Sieber said. "You'll be with me."

"Right."

"We'll leave tomorrow morning," Sieber said, "so say good-bye to whoever you have to say good-bye to."

"Just one person."

"A girl?"

"Yes."

"That figures," Sieber said. "I'll spend the rest of the day rounding up the rest of the men we'll be taking back with us."

"I don't think your young lieutenant is going to be happy about any of this."

"I know he's not," Sieber said, "but that's too bad. He'll do what Crook tells him to do."

"Speaking of which," Clint said, "what was the ace up Crook's sleeve?"

"What?"

"Oh, come on, Al," Clint said. "If you weren't able to talk me into this what was Crook's next play?"

"Well," Sieber said, touching his shirt pocket. Clint could hear paper crinkle inside. "I do have a telegram."

"From whom?"

"Washington."

"Yes, but from whom?"

Sieber looked at Clint and said, "The president of the United States."

"Asking for me?"

"Well," Sieber said, "he's not exactly *asking*. After all, he is the president."

"That's a pretty impressive ace," Clint said.

"I'm glad I didn't have to use it," Sieber said.

"So am I," Clint said.

"What would you have done?"

"You know," Clint said, "I'm not sure. I can get pretty stubborn sometimes."

"I think I remember that about you," Sieber said.

"What about supplies?" Clint asked.

"Just bring your horse and your guns," Al Sieber said. "The army will supply the rest."

"And am I getting paid for this?"

"I think," Sieber said, "you'll have to take that up with General Crook."

EIGHTEEN

Clint spent some time that day cleaning his rifle and pistol, making sure that they were in perfect working order. He then went to the livery and examined the gelding to make sure he was fit. The one kind of traveling that Duke's size was not ideal for was mountain traveling. Ideally a smaller horse, like Sieber's Indian pony, would have been better, but Clint wanted Duke's familiar presence beneath him on this trip.

Idly, during the course of the day, he wondered about Al Sieber's telegram. Was he telling the truth? Was there actually a missive from the president, possibly "ordering" Clint to come to the aid of his country? Or was that a bluff on Sieber's part?

No, Clint thought, no bluff. He had already agreed to help, so there had really been no reason for Sieber to lie about such a thing. There most likely was a telegram from the president. Clint wondered how stubborn he would have become if Sieber had actually tried to use it against him.

Crook believed in getting his way by whatever means he deemed necessary. This made the man a good soldier, and a good Indian fighter. The Crook that Clint remembered, though, did not have much in the way of a personality— outside of the service, that is—or a sense of humor.

Clint was glad that, technically speaking, he would not be under Crook's "command." This would enable him to bedevil the man a bit, if he wanted to.

And he had the feeling he was going to want to.

Clint ran into Sieber again that evening, in the saloon. He was sitting at the back table again, talking to Ginny, when Sieber approached the table. The girl gave him a dirty look and flounced away.

"That the girl?" Sieber asked, sitting and setting his beer on the table.

"That's her."

"She's mad at me."

"She's mad at me," Clint said.

"Oh."

"She *hates* you."

"Oh," Sieber said, in a different tone.

"Are we all set for tomorrow?" Clint asked.

Sieber nodded and took a moment to drink some of the cold beer. "Bowman and the other men will meet us at the livery in the morning," he said. "It'll take us the better part of two days to get to San Bernardino, since we'll be traveling with a fair-sized force and not riding at night."

"How many men will be with us?"

"About twelve."

"That's all? What will Crook's entire force be?"

"Let's see if I remember," Sieber said. "Nine officers, forty-two enlisted men, a hundred and ninety-three scouts—"

"A hundred and ninety-three?" Clint asked in surprise.

Sieber nodded.

"There'll be seventy-six civilian packers to handle the mules. The pack train is going to be a good-sized one, probably over two hundred."

"This force is not going to be moving with any speed, is it?" Clint asked.

"You and I and some of the others will be," Sieber said.

"We won't be staying with the main force."

"Glad to hear it," Clint said. "It sounds like you're going to present a pretty big target."

"Geronimo and Chatto don't have a lot of men, Clint," Sieber said. "Their raids are sort of like cyclones, coming in and then going out real quick. They're not likely to attack an army force."

"On second thought maybe I'd better stay—"

"You'll be with me," Sieber said. "I want your gun backing me up."

"Does that mean you're my boss?"

"That's an interesting question," Sieber said. "If you get Crook to put you on the payroll, *somebody* is gonna have to be your boss, either him or me."

"On the other hand?"

"On the other hand," Sieber said, "if you're a volunteer, then you'll be your own boss."

"Why do I get the idea you're trying to save the army some money?"

"Saving the army money ain't my job," Sieber said. "I just don't think you'll react well to somebody tryin' to give you orders."

"Al," Clint said seriously, "this is your baby. When we're in those mountains trying to catch up to Geronimo, trying to stay alive, it's your call."

"I knew you'd feel that way, Clint," Sieber said. He put his hand out and Clint took it and shook it. "Welcome aboard. I'm starting to think I might just come out of this alive."

"You and me both," Clint said.

Later that evening, still in the saloon, Ginny came over to his table.

"No poker tonight?" she asked.

"Not tonight."

"Are you gonna want to see me?"

"I think the question is," Clint said, "are you going to want to see me?"

"Well," she said, "if you're gonna go out and get yourself killed I think I'd better see you tonight, don't you? I mean, it might be my last chance."

"Ginny—"

She sat down across from him.

"You're goin', aren't you?"

"Yes."

"Why?"

"If for no other reason than to help my friend live through it," he said.

"Damn!" she snapped.

"What?"

"How can I argue with that?" she asked. "I thought you were gonna say somethin' like your country needs you, and then I'd say your country could get along without you very well. No, you've got to tell me about keepin' your friend alive."

"That's my main reason."

"I have to get back to work," she said.

As she stood up he asked, "Wasn't this supposed to be your day off?"

"It was," she said, "but I came in. I'd be driving myself crazy thinking about you going into the mountains, and worryin' about you gettin' killed. This is better for me." She put her hand on his arm. "I'll see you after work."

"I'll be here," he said.

"We can say good-bye proper."

Whether he got killed or not Clint was starting to think that saying good-bye was a good idea.

NINETEEN

Clint met up with Sieber in front of the livery early the next morning and together they waited until Bowman appeared with eleven other men—eight soldiers, two scouts. There were also two pack mules, and one handler.

"Glad you're comin' with us, Clint," Bowman said. "Sorry about the other day."

"That's okay, Sam," Clint said. "You were just following orders, looking me over."

"Let's get started," Sieber said. "We got a lot of miles to cover, and we ain't gonna be movin' all that fast."

"Think we'll run into them redskins?" one of the soldiers asked. He had one stripe on his sleeve, as did most of the men. In fact, the highest-ranking soldier was a corporal, and Clint thought he recognized him.

"You never know," Sieber said to the private. "Just get in the habit of keeping your eyes open."

"I know you, don't I?" Clint asked the corporal.

"Uh, yessir."

"That's right," Clint said, "you were following me."

"I was only followin' orders, sir."

"At ease, soldier," Clint said. "No hard feelings."

"Thank you, sir."

"Let's move out," Sieber said again. "You girls can talk along the way."

Sieber led the way out of town, with Clint behind him, then Bowman, and then the soldiers strung out with the mule handler bringing up the rear.

When they cleared the town Clint moved up to ride alongside Sieber.

"Tell me about Geronimo."

"From what I can see he's a born leader who doesn't like the way his people are being treated on the reservation."

"A born leader and he only got, what, twenty men to follow him?"

"A lot of the Apaches want to stay on the reservation, Clint," Sieber said. "At least, that's what I think. Crook says they're lazy."

"What do you think?"

"Me?" Sieber said. "I think they're tired, just plumb wore out. They're lookin' for a place to settle down and spend their last years."

"So it's the young ones following Geronimo?"

"For the most part, but Geronimo is no kid himself. By the white man's calender I reckon he's close to sixty."

"Then why isn't he tired, like the others?"

"He's tired, all right," Sieber said, "but he's also stubborn as a mule, and independent as hell.

"Chatto's younger than Geronimo, and headstrong as hell," Sieber said. "He's been a member of Geronimo's band of Chiricahuas for years, but now he's taken on a band of his own, a lot of the young ones."

"So he and Geronimo are not adversaries."

"Not at all," Sieber said, "we're the adversaries. They've simply split their forces to cover more ground, wreak more havoc."

"How long does Crook think it will take to round them up, once he gets permission to cross the border?"

"I'm not privy to the general's timetable," Sieber said. "I'm only a civilian scout. You want to ask him a question like that, that's up to you."

"I will."

Sieber glanced at Clint for a moment, then looked straight ahead again.

"You gonna give him a hard time?"

"What makes you ask that?" Clint asked.

"The two of you don't seem to have very high opinions of each other."

"Is that a fact?" Clint said. "What's he say about me?"

"He thinks you're rude and insolent," Sieber said. "At least, that's what he remembers about you. How many times have you two met?"

"Once, and it was at a party," Clint said, "and the general was pontificating loudly about Indians and Indian fighting. His opinions were not ones held by many others, but that didn't seem to matter to him."

"It wouldn't."

"He might be a great Indian fighter, a great soldier and tactician," Clint said, "but his command of *tact* leaves something to be desired."

"And you told him so?"

"In no uncertain terms."

"That explains his opinion, then."

"So why does he want me?"

"He respects you," Sieber said.

"My reputation?"

"No," the scout said, "you."

"You mean he's able to look past the reputation?" Clint asked.

"Crook is not impressed by stories, Clint," Sieber said.

"Have you told him stories?"

"I've told him facts."

"So does *he* want me," Clint asked, "or was it you?"

Sieber looked at him briefly again, then turned his eyes forward.

"A little bit of both, I guess."

TWENTY

When they camped that night Clint took care of Duke
and looked around at the absolute military precision that
was taking place. By the time he was done all of the other
horses and mules had been picketed, a fire had been made,
food was cooking, and watches had been set.

"I'm impressed," Clint said to Sieber as he joined him
by the fire. Sieber poured out a cup of coffee and handed
it to him.

"Don't be," the scout replied. "This is easy. The hard
part comes when we come face-to-face with Geronimo. I'll
be impressed when I see how they react when they're being
shot at."

"Geronimo and his people have guns?"

Sieber nodded.

"Winchesters," he said, "and they know how to use
them."

"I'm sure your men do, too."

"They're not my men," Sieber said, "they're Crook's
men, and they know how to shoot at targets that don't shoot
back."

"I get the feeling you're going into this whole thing with
the wrong attitude."

"Well, I was."

"You mean me? How can I make that much of a difference?"

"I've seen you shoot, Clint."

"Okay, I can hit what I shoot at."

"Every time," Sieber said, "more accurately and faster than any man I've ever seen."

"I've only got so many bullets, Al," Clint said. "What's really going on here?"

"I gave you my motives," Sieber said. "For anything else you'll have to talk to Crook."

The two men watched as the men moved around the camp. The mule handler turned out to also be the cook. Clint was glad the man didn't try anything fancier than beans.

Bowman joined Sieber and Clint to eat, while the other men broke into several different groups. Clint noticed that the corporal was sitting alone.

"What's his name?" he asked.

"Whose?" Bowman replied.

"The two-striper."

"That's Watkins, I think," Bowman said. "Yeah, Evan Watkins."

"He's young."

"Young to be a corporal," Bowman said. "That's why he's eatin' alone."

"That doesn't seem right," Clint said. "You earn your stripes and lose your friends because you outrank them now?"

"That's the way it is," Bowman said.

"Well, if you boys will excuse me," Clint said, "I'll just go over and keep the young man company."

"Go ahead," Sieber said.

"We'll try to get along without you," Bowman said.

Clint took his plate and his cup and walked across the camp to where Corporal Watkins was sitting.

"Mind if I join you, Corporal?"

"Oh," Watkins said, looking up at Clint in surprise, "no, sir, sit right down."

"Thanks."

Clint sat down a few feet from the younger man and got comfortable.

"You don't have to call me sir, you know," he said. "I'm not in the army, and I'm not your superior."

"If you don't mind, uh, sir," Watkins said, "it's just out of respect for who you are."

"You know who I am?"

"Oh, yes, sir."

"That's right," Clint said, "you were tailing me."

"Just doing my jo—"

"I know you were doing your job, son," Clint said. "I already told you, there's no need to apologize."

"Yes, sir. Sorry, uh, I mean—"

"Never mind."

Suddenly, from across the camp, came the laughter of several men and Watkins looked over at them.

"Wish you were eating with your friends, Corporal?" Clint asked.

"Oh, they ain't my friends," the corporal said, "leastways, not anymore."

"Because of those?" Clint asked, indicating the man's stripes.

Watkins shrugged and said, "I guess."

"Are those stripes worth losing friends?"

"I figure if they let these stripes stop us from bein' friends, they wasn't really my friends, anyway."

"Well, that seems to be a healthy way to look at it."

" 'Sides," Watkins said, "I plan to get more stripes than this, and I can't be worried about losing friends while I move up in the ranks."

"How far up do you plan to move?"

"As far as I can get," Watkins said. "Maybe all the way."

"To president?"

"I don't want to be the president," Watkins said, "just a general."

"It's nice to meet a young man who knows what he wants to do."

"Did you know what you wanted, sir?" Watkins asked. "When you was my age?"

"I thought I did," Clint said, "but as it turns out, Corporal, I had no idea at all what I was getting myself into."

TWENTY-ONE

They moved out the next morning without incident.

"I don't think we'll be seeing Geronimo or Chatto this far back from the border," Bowman said.

"I agree," Sieber said.

"Well, I have no opinion," Clint said. "I'll just have to rely on your experience."

"If you don't mind me askin' . . ." Bowman said.

"Asking what?"

"What was Quanah Parker like?"

"That was years ago, Sam," Clint said. "He was like any strong-willed young man, Indian or white. He demanded respect, and what he thought was rightfully his."

"And if he didn't get it," Al Sieber said, "he took it by force."

"The way his people had been doing it for years," Clint said. "It's the way they were raised."

"Is it true his mother was white?" Bowman asked.

"Oh, yes, that is true," Clint said. "She was stolen as a young woman and grew up among the Comanches. When she was 'rescued' and taken 'home' she was treated miserably. The poor woman didn't really belong in either world."

"Those bastards!" Bowman said.

"Who, Sam?" Clint asked. "Who were the bastards? The men who stole her the first time, or the men who stole her the second time?"

"But . . . you said she was rescued."

"It's a word," Clint said. "Rescued is just a word. She was taken away from the only world she ever really knew."

"With the Comanches?"

"She had gotten married, and she had children," Clint said. "She should have been left there."

"I think any woman who's stolen by the Indians should be rescued, no matter when."

"Well, the next time you find a white woman among the Indians and you want to rescue her," Clint said, "try asking her first. See what she says."

Bowman looked at Clint as if he didn't understand, but Clint was tired of talking about it. He looked at Sieber, who gave him only a cursory glance, one he couldn't read, and kept his opinion to himself.

"There's the camp," Sieber said, pointing into the distance. "We made good time."

It would be dark within the hour, so Clint had to agree, they had made very good time.

"I don't think Crook is there."

"Why not?"

"There's too much activity," Sieber said. "When he's around the men try to stay quiet and not move around that much."

"Why?"

"They don't want him to notice them."

"If he's not there," Clint asked, "who's in command?"

"Captain Bourke."

"How does he get along with the men?"

"Not so great," Sieber said. "He's a Crook crony."

"Crook crony?" Clint repeated.

"That's what the men call the officers who are trying to please Crook," Bowman said, "or be just like him."

"I see."

"We'd better ride in before it gets dark," Sieber said. "Let's go."

As they approached the camp a sentry approached them, took a good look, and then let them pass.

"Is the general in camp?" Sieber called out to the man.

"No, he's not."

"Corporal?" Sieber called out.

Corporal Evan Watkins came riding up and reined his horse in beside Sieber.

"Yes, sir?"

"You take the men into camp and get them settled, and then report to Captain Bourke."

"Yes, sir."

"And don't call me 'sir.' "

"Yes, si—uh, okay."

Watkins turned and called out instructions to the men. Clint watched with interest to see if the men obeyed him, and they did. Maybe they weren't friends anymore, but they respected the extra stripe.

Clint, Sieber, Bowman, the two other scouts, and the mule handler allowed the soldiers to proceed ahead of them, and then followed.

"When we get into camp I'll introduce you to Captain Bourke," Sieber said.

"Okay."

"After that you'll be on your own to meet the rest of the officers."

"Fine."

"I think you'll be able to pick out all of the Crook cronies for yourself."

Clint was looking forward to it.

TWENTY-TWO

When they rode into camp a soldier came up to Sieber and took his horse.

"We can have somebody take care of your horse while I introduce you to the captain," the scout told Clint.

"It'd better be someone who's good with horses, or he'll lose a finger," Clint said.

"I think I can handle it, sir," the soldier who had taken Sieber's horse said.

Clint looked at Sieber.

"He can handle mine, and that's not easy. Give him a try."

"Okay," Clint said, handing the man Duke's reins, "it's your funeral."

He was surprised as hell when Duke walked off docile as you please with the man.

"What's his name?" he asked.

"Riley," Sieber said. "Can't hit a thing with a rifle, but he can talk to horses, and they seem to talk back."

"I guess so," Clint said.

"This way," Sieber said. "I'd be willing to bet that Captain Bourke is in General Crook's tent."

Sure enough, that was where they found the captain.

"This here's Clint Adams, Captain," Sieber said as they entered the tent. "Captain Bourke, Clint."

"Captain," Clint said, extending his hand, but although the captain stood up he made no move to accept the handshake.

Bourke was in his late thirties, maybe even forty. Clint had the feeling that this was a man who was walking the edge between being stuck as a captain for too long or moving up to the next level.

"I might as well tell you right now, Adams, that I wasn't in favor of you coming here."

"Well," Clint said, withdrawing his hand, "this wasn't my first choice either, Captain."

"Yes, I see," Bourke said. "General Crook filled me in on your . . . background, Adams."

"Oh? Knows all about it, does he?"

"He knows enough," Bourke said, "and he told me enough. This is no place for a gunfighter."

"I agree," Clint said.

"Then why did you come?"

"Because I'm not a gunfighter," Clint said. "Because Al Sieber is a friend of mine and he asked me to come."

"I see," Bourke said. "You didn't come because General Crook asked for you?"

"No."

"And you didn't come to serve your country?"

Clint snorted and said, "No," and the captain bristled.

"I see General Crook was right about your irreverence," he said.

"Nice to see the general was right about something."

"And your insubordination."

"Right again."

"He can't be insubordinate, Captain," Sieber said, "because he's not under your command."

Bourke looked at Sieber and said, "I think I'd like to talk to Mr. Adams alone, Mr. Sieber."

Sieber looked at Clint, who nodded, and the scout withdrew from the tent.

"What's on your mind, Captain?" Clint asked.

"General Crook wants you here, Mr. Adams," Bourke said. "I have no recourse but to go along with that, but I want you to know that I'll have my eye on you. I'll—"

He was cut off by Clint's laughter.

"What do you find so funny?" the captain demanded.

"You, Captain," Clint said. "I find you funny. If Crook was here I wouldn't take any shit from him, what makes you think I'll take any from you? Your little speech about keeping your eye on me is ludicrous. Keep your eye on me? For what? I'm here to help, Captain, I'm not some raw recruit who's going to go over the hill. Keep your eye on me. You're just trying to flex some muscles here that, in my opinion, you don't even have."

Clint turned and walked to the tent flap, then turned back.

"When General Crook gets back I'll talk to him," he said, "but for now, I think you and I had better stay out of each other's way, don't you?"

Clint held the captain's gaze just long enough to determine that the man had nothing else to say, then turned and left.

TWENTY-THREE

"What happened?" Sieber asked as Clint came out of the tent.

"We came to an understanding."

"What kind of an understanding?"

"He'll stay out of my way and I'll stay out of his until Crook gets back."

"I think he has that understanding with a lot of people," Sieber said.

"Because he's a Crook crony?" Clint asked.

"He just wants to be Crook," Sieber said. "Look, I've got to pull my scouts together and talk to them. I think we're gonna have to be ready to move when Crook gets back."

"Okay," Clint said, "I'll see you later."

As Sieber walked away Clint turned and looked at Crook's tent and saw Corporal Earl Watkins going in. He felt sorry for Watkins. The young man was going to have to pay the price for Clint's "insubordinate" behavior. He decided to wait for the man to come out and then try to console him.

Sure enough, when the young corporal reappeared minutes later he had a long face, but to his credit he also looked angry.

"Can I buy you a cup of coffee?" Clint asked.

Watkins looked around, then spotted Clint and came over.

"Where?"

"I don't know," Clint said, looking around camp. "There are a few fires in camp, there must be coffee somewhere. Let's find it."

"Sounds good to me."

They started to walk together.

"The captain lit into you, huh?"

"Guess he had a burr under his saddle," Watkins said, "but I don't know why he had to take it out on me."

"Makes you mad, doesn't it?"

"Yessir, it does," Watkins said. "I don't consider it proper behavior for an officer."

"You'd never act that way?"

"No, sir."

"Never treat a young soldier that way?"

"No."

"So I guess you're going to be a good officer."

"You can bet on it."

"Well, then, you'll have to be different."

"I am different."

They walked a few feet and the young man asked, "How different?"

"You'll have to be one of the ones who doesn't let the bars get to him, change him. Haven't you noticed how men change when they become officers? Well, look at you, for instance. You've got an extra stripe now."

"It hasn't changed me."

"No, but it has changed the way others look at you, hasn't it? The way they act around you?"

"I guess so."

"You know so."

"Yes, I do."

"Well," Clint said, "it's ten times worse with bars, lieutenant's, captain's, and on up."

They reached a fire that had a coffeepot on it. Clint asked a soldier if they could have some coffee. He was a young man, a private, and he said, "Sure thing," and gave them each a cup.

"Thank you," Corporal Watkins said to the private, who gave him a funny look.

"See?" Clint asked.

"See what?"

"You outrank him, and yet you thanked him for the coffee. That puzzled him. He's not used to being treated that way by a superior."

"I'm not a superior—"

"Yes, you are," Clint said. "That extra stripe makes you superior to him."

Watkins looked down at the stripes on his arm, as if they suddenly held new meaning for him.

"You're starting to get it, aren't you?"

"I understand," Watkins said, "but I'm still not gonna change."

"Well, then, good for you, soldier," Clint said. "You'll be one of the different ones."

Clint finished his coffee and handed it back to the private.

"Thanks, soldier."

"Sure thing."

As Clint walked away, Watkins walked over to where the other soldier was and started talking to him, as if neither of them had *any* stripes on their arms.

Maybe, Clint thought, he would be different.

Clint went to check on Duke and the soldier who had taken him. He found the man brushing the big gelding, and Duke was standing still and taking it.

"I don't believe it," Clint said.

The soldier looked over his shoulder and said, "Oh, hello, sir. This is a fine animal."

"Yes, he is," Clint said.

"Um, sir, can I ask you a question?"

"Sure, go ahead."

"Are you Clint Adams?"

"Yes, I am."

"We heard you might be coming to join up with us," the man said. "I was wondering if you'd be bringing your horse. Duke, right?"

"That's right."

"I've heard a lot about him," the soldier said. "I really get along well with horses."

"I can see that," Clint said. "I'm impressed. He doesn't usually let anyone brush him without putting up a fuss first."

"Oh, he didn't put up a fuss," Private Riley said. "All I had to do was talk to him some, that's all. We came to an understanding."

"Well, that's good," Clint said. "That's real good."

"Do you want to finish him up?" Riley asked, offering Clint the brush.

"No, no," Clint said, "you're doing a fine job. Keep going."

The man nodded and went back to his task.

Riley seemed typical of the men who were in camp. Most of them seemed young and inexperienced. Clint wondered why Crook was not able to get a regiment of more experienced men for this job.

If most of them were like Riley and Watkins, they would probably grow into good soldiers. All they'd have to do to accomplish that was survive this encounter with Geronimo and his men.

TWENTY-FOUR

Clint spent most of his time with the scouts because, like he, they were not soldiers. Soldiers had a totally different thought process than did scouts—and certainly different than Clint, who had never been one for taking orders.

"And blindly," he added.

"What?" Sieber asked.

"The army expects you to blindly take orders."

"Like Custer's men," Bowman said.

"Exactly," Clint said. "That's a great example. How many of those men do you think knew they were going to die, but had to follow Custer because he was their superior?"

"Lots of them?" Bowman said.

"Right."

"I guess that's why I never became a soldier," Sieber said. "I won't follow anyone blindly."

"Me, either," Bowman said.

The three of them were sitting around a fire which they had started and so, consequently, did not have to share it with anyone else.

"I never knew a man I'd follow blindly," Sieber went on, "soldier or no."

"What about you, Clint?"

"I've known some men I would back in almost any situation," Clint said. "Men who would back me, if the reason was good enough."

"If you were in the right?" Bowman asked.

"Right or wrong has nothing to do with it," Clint said. "You only need to give a good enough reason and the right people will back you."

"Name one," Sieber said.

"Hickok," Clint said without hesitation. "Bat Masterson's another. No matter what situation I was in Hickok would back me—Masterson still will."

"Can you get him here in a hurry?" Bowman asked.

"Even if I could, I wouldn't," Clint said.

"Your reason for being here not good enough?" Sieber asked.

"You tell me, Al," Clint said. "You're the reason I'm here. That president's telegram sure wouldn't have been reason enough."

"What telegram?" Bowman asked.

"General Crook arranged for the president himself to request Clint's help," Sieber said to Bowman. "Only Clint agreed to do it before I could show him the telegram."

"Really?" Bowman asked. "From the president himself?"

"That's right," Sieber said.

"Can I see it?" Bowman asked.

"Can you read?" Sieber asked.

"Not very well."

"Then why do you want to see it?"

"I ain't never seen nothin' that came from the president."

"Show it to him, Al," Clint said.

"How come you never asked to see it?" Sieber asked Clint.

"I didn't need to," Clint said. "It didn't figure into my decision."

"I would have thought, just out of curiosity . . ." Sieber

said. "Or, maybe, just to see if it really existed."

"I took your word for that, Al," Clint said. "Your word is good enough for me."

"Good."

"But you could show it to Sam," Clint said. "Where's the harm?"

"Yeah," Bowman said, "where's the harm?"

Sieber sighed and said, "Well, if you really want to see it."

"I do."

Sieber reached into his shirt pocket and then frowned. He patted some other pockets, still frowning.

"What's the matter?" Bowman asked.

"Can't seem to find it."

"You lost it?"

"No, I didn't lose it," Sieber said, "I probably just . . . misplaced it."

"Ah, shit," Bowman said, "I really wanted to see that, Al."

"Well, come by my tent later and I'll see if I can find it." As Chief of Scouts Sieber rated his own tent. "You, too, if you like," he said to Clint.

"How many times do I have to tell you, I take your word for it, Al?"

"I just thought, since I couldn't find it now, you might think . . ."

"That you lied?"

Sieber didn't say anything.

"Would you have lied to get me out here, Al?"

"That's a good question," Sieber said. "I'm not sure I know the answer, Clint."

"Well, I do," Clint said. "If you thought it was important enough you'd lie to your mother."

"You know that and you still came out?" Sieber asked. "Why?"

Clint waited a moment, then said, "You know what? I'm not all that sure I can answer that one."

TWENTY-FIVE

The next morning Al Sieber woke Clint by shaking him violently.

"What the hell—" Clint complained.

"Get up," Sieber said. "Crook will be here in a matter of hours."

"Who says?"

"He sent a scout ahead," Sieber said. "He wants his officers ready, as well as me and you."

"Is that a fact?"

"Don't start, Clint," Sieber said. "Just do me a favor and get up . . . please."

Clint got up without further word. In fact, he talked to no one until he'd had a cup of coffee.

There was much activity in the camp, in anticipation of the arrival of their commander. Capt. Bourke was yelling orders at the soldiers, who were scampering around doing who knew what, because Clint sure didn't know. What was there to be done? What was Crook going to do, come back and inspect the camp? He had other things on his mind.

Sieber came over while Clint was having his second cup of coffee.

"Want one?" he asked.

"Sure, why not?"

He poured Sieber a cup and handed it to him.

"What's the word?" Clint asked.

"The scout says Crook got permission to cross the border," Sieber said.

"So we'll be moving soon."

"Tomorrow's May first," Sieber said. "That's when Crook wanted to move, so I guess that's when we'll be movin'."

"Is everybody ready?"

"They better be."

He watched as a group of privates scurried about policing the area.

"Why does Bourke have them cleaning the area?" Clint asked.

"Crook's a clean freak," Sieber said. "He's almost compulsive about it."

Clint didn't know what Sieber's education was, and he was sometimes surprised at the way the man talked. Half the time he sounded like he was from the mountains, and the other half you'd swear he'd been educated in the East. "Clean freak" was not a phrase Clint heard often, and neither was the word "compulsive" one that was in the vocabulary of most Westerners.

"He's going to worry about that when he's got Geronimo on his mind?"

"Bourke's just being careful," Sieber said. "He doesn't want to get on Crook's wrong side. None of us do."

"Including me?"

"Especially you," Sieber said. "You're one of the first ones he's gonna want to see when he gets here."

Clint ran a hand over his face and said, "I'll be awake by then. Where can I wash up?"

"I'll have some water brought over," Sieber said, then studied Clint's face carefully and added, "and a razor."

Later, after Clint was washed and shaved, Sieber came over and said, "Crook's back."

"I know," Clint said. "I saw."

"He's back in his tent, and he wants to see you. Are you ready?"

"Sure."

"Are you gonna behave?"

"I will if he does," Clint said.

"Clint—"

"You have a lot of respect for him, don't you?" Clint asked, interrupting him.

"Yes," Sieber said, then added, "I have a lot of respect for the both of you."

"Okay," Clint said, after a moment, "lead the way. I'll behave."

When they reached Crook's tent Sieber went in first, then came back out and got Clint.

"General Crook," he said as they entered the tent together, "Clint Adams. I believe you gents have met before."

Crook stood up from behind his desk. He was white-haired, his skin dark from hours of exposure to the sun. He wasn't tall, but he was imposing.

"Mr. Adams," Crook said, "I'm glad you were able to make it."

"I'm here to help, if I can, sir," Clint said.

"That's . . . commendable," Crook said. "Uh, Mr. Sieber . . ."

Al Sieber stepped forward, produced a telegram from his pocket, and passed it to the general.

"There was no need for it, sir."

"Indeed?" Crook said, obviously surprised. He read the telegram, then looked at Clint. "Do you know what this is?"

"I have an idea."

"Mr. Sieber did not show you this?"

"No, sir."

"Before you made your decision?"

"Not before," Clint said, "nor since, sir."

"I must say, Mr. Adams," Crook said, "you're quite . . . different from the way you were the last time we saw each other."

"So are you, sir," Clint said. "But those were different circumstances, weren't they?"

"Yes," Crook said thoughtfully, "yes, they were, weren't they?"

"Sir," Clint said, and looked at Sieber, who was staring at him with a look that said "thank you."

Clint was curious to see how long all this civility was going to last.

TWENTY-SIX

"Have a seat, Mr. Adams," Crook said, seating himself behind his field desk.

Clint pulled over an extra field chair and sat.

"Has Mr. Sieber told you what is expected of you?" Crook asked.

"I'm not sure Al knows what's expected of me, General."

"Well, then, I must confess," Crook said, "I'm not entirely sure of that myself. When I heard you were . . . available . . . it just seemed a prudent move to secure your services."

"I see."

"I know your reputation with a gun, of course, but I also know that reputations are often exaggerated."

"There are many aspects of my reputation that are exaggerated, General, but even I have to say that that is not one of them. I am very good with a gun."

"Amazingly good, is what I heard."

"Perhaps that, too."

"Then you'll be a valuable man to have."

"May I ask some questions, General?" Clint asked. "I mean, since we're talking about reputations."

"By all means."

"I've heard you called the greatest living Indian fighter."

To his credit Crook looked embarrassed.

"I've heard that one, too."

"Are you here to fight Geronimo and his men, or to get them to go back to the reservation?"

"That's a good question, Mr. Adams," Crook said. "My first goal is, of course, to entice them back to the reservation without bloodshed."

"I'm glad to hear it."

"But failing that," Crook went on, "my orders are to put an end to their raiding by any means."

"I see."

Crook sat forward in his chair, placed one elbow on the desk, and said, "I fully intend to follow my orders, Mr. Adams."

"I'd expect no less of you, sir," Clint said. "I'm here to help in any way I can."

"I think we understand each other, Mr. Adams."

"I hope so, General."

As if to make his point Crook stood up and held out his hand. Clint stood and shook it.

"Welcome."

"Thank you, sir."

"You'll be riding with Mr. Sieber and myself, Mr. Adams," Crook said, "and whoever else I decide to take with us. No matter what happens, though, you, Mr. Sieber, and I will be inseparable. That means if I have a meeting with Geronimo, you will both accompany me."

"I'm honored, General."

"Wait until this is all over to tell me you were honored to be involved in any of it, sir," Crook said. "We'll speak again before tomorrow."

Clint took that as a dismissal, turned and left.

"What was that all about?" Sieber asked.

"What?"

"The two of you being so civil to each other," the scout

said. "If I didn't know better I'd say you . . . you respected each other."

"We've only had one other meeting, Al," Clint said, "and that was under very different circumstances. To tell you the truth, I think we were both drunk that night."

"Crook? Drunk?"

"Maybe just a little."

"I would have loved to see that."

"Mr. Sieber?"

They both turned to see Captain Bourke standing there.

"Yes?"

"General Crook would like to see you and Mr. Bowman," Bourke said.

"Tell the general I'll find Bowman and we'll be right in."

Bourke didn't like being a messenger boy, neither from Crook to Sieber or the other way around, that was clear.

"I'll tell him," he finally said, and withdrew.

"He sings a different tune when the general is around, huh?" Clint asked.

"Bourke is not even a Crook crony," Sieber said, "he's just a yes-man. I have no respect for him at all."

"Naturally," Clint said, "that probably means he'll be going along with us."

"Who's us?" Sieber asked.

"You, me, and the general."

"Is this something I should know?" Sieber asked.

Clint grinned and said, "Maybe that's what he wants to tell you and Bowman."

"Bowman," Sieber said, as if reminded that he had to find the man. "I'll talk to you later, Clint."

"Enjoy your meeting."

Sieber scowled and went off in search of Sam Bowman. Clint walked back to the fire he shared with the two scouts and got himself a cup of coffee. Going over Crook's words in his head, he wondered if the general was going to use

him as a kind of bodyguard. Actually, Clint wouldn't mind
that job. The army seemed to think that Crook was the man
to solve this particular problem, and there were worse jobs
than trying to keep him alive.

TWENTY-SEVEN

Throughout the course of the evening Clint met some of the others who would be accompanying General Crook into Mexico.

The first was a man named A. Frank Randall, a correspondent of the *New York Herald*. Clint met him when Randall, a fussy man who had no business being in the West, let alone on a trek like this, approached him carrying photographic equipment, while he was seated at the fire, drinking coffee.

"Excuse me?"

"Yes."

The man put his equipment down, then approached Clint and extended his hand.

"A. Frank Randall," he said, "the *New York Herald*."

"Hello," Clint said, shaking the man's hand.

"I understand you are Clint Adams?"

"That's right."

"I have been sent here by my editor to cover this . . . this campaign of General Crook and could not believe my luck when I heard you were present."

"And why is that?"

"Because, sir," Randall said, "you are the Gunsmith.

103

You are a legend, and General Crook—if not already so—
is also on his way to becoming a legend.''

"Is that a fact?"

"It is, indeed, sir," Randall said. "Now, if you would
just remain sitting there until I set up my equipment . . ."
He scurried over to his photographic equipment and began
to set it up.

Clint stood and dumped the remains of his coffee into
the fire, which flared in protest.

"No," he said.

"Sir?" Randall said, looking over his shoulder and, consequently, losing control of his equipment, which fell over.
Clint doubted the man would ever get the camera into the
mountains in one piece.

"No photos."

"But, sir—" Randall didn't know whether to pick up
the equipment or pursue Clint, who had started to walk
away. He finally decided on Clint.

"But, sir, I am here with the blessing of the United States
Army, and General Crook. They wish us to—"

"Look," Clint said, whirling on the man so quickly that
Randall almost fell over in his haste to stop, "maybe Crook
wants his photo taken, and if he does, that's fine with me,
but I don't. Do you understand? I . . . do . . . not!"

With that he turned and walked away from the newspa-
perman and almost walked right into another man.

"Hey!" the man said.

"Sorry," Clint said, "I'm sorry. I'm just trying to get
away from a . . . a pest."

"Pest," the man said. "That could only be A. Frank
Randall."

"Exactly."

The man stuck out his hand. He was tall, and tanned,
and bearded.

"Name's Mickey Free."

"Clint Adams."

"I know," Free said, "I heard you were with us."

"Are you a scout, Mickey?" Clint asked. "I thought most of the scouts except for Sieber and Bowman were Indians?"

"I'm an interpreter," Free said.

Clint obviously looked surprised.

"I know what you're thinking," Free said. "I'm half-Irish and half-Mexican, but when I was eleven or twelve I was given to the White Mountain Apaches, and they brought me up."

"I see."

"Is that coffee I smell?" Free asked.

"I've got a pot on the fire, if that pest has gone away."

Clint turned to have a look and, sure enough, Randall had managed to drag away all his equipment.

"Don't mind if I do," Free said, and started for the fire.

Although Free had invited himself for coffee, Clint found him to be an affable man, full of stories about his childhood and more recent incidents.

He told Clint about the Indian called "Peaches."

"There he is," he said, pointing across the camp. Clint saw an odd-looking Apache who, although full-blooded, had a fair complexion and rosy cheeks.

"Supposed to be full-blooded," Free said, "but there's got to be some white in his past, wouldn't you say?"

"I would," Clint said, "or else where did that complexion come from?"

"Exactly."

Free went on to tell Clint that the man's real name was Tsoe. He was captured with a bunch of renegades, and Tsoe was among them, but he managed to convince Crook that he had simply been "visiting" some relatives. As it turned out, Tsoe was a congenial sort, friendly, generally truthful, and very cooperative. When Crook asked him to become a scout the man heartily agreed.

"It is his knowledge of the terrain that will be most

useful,'' Free said. ''But look at the fucker. Ain't he the finest lookin' man you ever saw?''

It was an odd remark, but Clint immediately saw that it was true. Tsoe, or ''Peaches,'' was possibly the handsomest man he'd ever seen.

''He never gets tired, and I've never seen him annoyed or in a bad humor,'' Free said. ''If we had any women here they would be all over him.''

Free finished his coffee and returned the cup to Clint.

''Well, I've got to get ready for tomorrow,'' Free said. ''I'm glad we ran into each other and had a chance to talk.''

''See you tomorrow,'' Clint said.

Free left and walked off to make whatever preparations he had to for the next day. Clint decided to check on Duke one more time, after which he'd check his guns, and then his own preparations would be done.

TWENTY-EIGHT

The next day they began their march down the San Bernardino River. A. Frank Randall referred to it as an "expedition."

Many of the scouts moved on ahead, but there was not much to see. In the wake of their raids the Apaches had left destruction and fear. For three days' march they saw no one. Land formerly cultivated for growth was now overgrown with cane and mesquite. Some of the towns they came to were long abandoned.

They reached the Bavispe and moved through the canyon, coming to river towns like San Miguel, Bavispe, and Huachinera. The people there greeted them with great joy, feeling that they were being delivered from the hands of the Apaches.

The condition of the towns was terrible. No one ventured away from their homes, for fear of running into the Apaches, whose raids came without warning.

After a week they were camped near an abandoned ranch called Tesorababi, which had been abandoned because of the raids.

Sitting around one fire was Clint, Al Sieber, Sam Bowman, and Mickey Free.

"Tomorrow," Sieber said, "we move into their territory. The general's tired of fooling around."

"Do we know where they are?" Clint asked.

"Not exactly," Sieber said, "but they're leaving sign."

"What kind of sign?" Clint asked. "I thought Apaches could move around without leaving sign."

"You'll see tomorrow," Sieber said.

"I'll be moving ahead with some of the scouts tomorrow," Bowman said. "We'll be sending back messages about routes and likely campsites."

"You and I will be staying with Crook," Sieber said to Clint.

"How many scouts will be moving ahead?" Clint asked.

"A hundred and fifty," Bowman said.

Clint's eyes widened and he said, "That many?"

"There are a lot of trails in the mountains," Bowman said, "plus, like I said, we'll be sending messengers back. A hundred and fifty will just about do it."

"Gentlemen," someone said.

They all looked up and saw Frank Randall standing with his equipment.

"A photograph?" he asked eagerly.

Clint and Mickey Free both said, "No!" at the same time.

"I guess not, Frankie," Sieber said.

"Well, then," Randall said, "an interview?"

"Not with me," Clint said.

"Or me," Mickey said.

"Sam," Al said, "why don't you give the man an interview?"

"Why?"

"The old man wants us to cooperate with the press," Sieber said.

"Well, okay," Bowman said. He stood up and walked over to the journalist. "Let's go for a walk, Frankie, and you can tell me what you want to know."

"Can I take *your* picture, Mr. Bowman?"

"Sure, Frankie," Bowman said, looking over his shoulder at the others, "why not? I'm better lookin' than any of those guys, anyway."

As Bowman walked Clint asked, "What about Peaches? Where's he going to be?"

"He'll be with us," Sieber said. "He knows where one of Geronimo's camps was. He's gonna take us there tomorrow."

"An old camp?"

"More than likely," Sieber said. "Geronimo and his men keep movin' around."

"They've sure done a lot of damage for a few men," Clint said.

"Apaches," Mickey Free said, "think that each of them is worth ten white men."

"What do you think?" Clint asked.

Free looked at Sieber and laughed.

"I think that's a conservative estimate," he said, and then added, "present company excepted, of course."

"Of course," Clint said.

"I've got to set the watches," Sieber said, standing up. "You fellas better bed down for the night. I'll see you in the morning."

Sieber walked away, and Clint and Mickey Free shared one last cup of coffee before turning in.

"Any White Mountain Apaches with Geronimo, Mickey?" Clint asked.

"Could be some," Mickey said.

"Some you know?"

"Maybe."

"Do you think Crook will be able to get Geronimo to come in peacefully?"

"I'll tell you something about Geronimo, Clint," Mickey said. "He's a reasonable man. You can talk to him. It's gonna depend on what Crook has to say."

"And what about Chatto?"

The look on Mickey's face changed.

"What about him?"

"Is he reasonable?" Clint asked. "Can he be talked to?"

"No," Mickey said, shaking his head. "Chatto's a hot-head. We only have one thing going for us with him."

"What's that?"

"Up to now he's listened to Geronimo."

"So if Geronimo says he's going back to the reservation, Chatto will go, too?"

Mickey tossed the remnants of his coffee into the fire, looked at Clint, and said, "Maybe."

TWENTY-NINE

The next day Clint found out what Sieber had meant when he'd said the Apaches were leaving sign behind. They had cached most of what they had stolen—or hunted—in the trees. Sieber pointed and Clint saw dried meats, mescal, cowhides, horsehides, buckskin, as well as cloth, actual clothing, saddles, flour, other food supplies and, in one instance, letters they had stolen.

Peaches located the camp he remembered, and it was abandoned. Even Clint could see that the ground had been trampled down by many feet, as well as animals. On the summit of a mountain they found forty lodges, and in another place thirty, all abandoned. In every nook and cranny there seemed to be something left behind.

"Why take everything if they're going to leave it behind?" Clint asked at one point.

"They take as much as they can," Sieber said, "use as much of it as they can, then leave the rest behind and move on. They travel light."

At one point, coming down the other side of a mountain, they found an open area that had obviously been used as a camp. There were the frames of hurriedly dismantled wickiups, the straw of abandoned beds, mescal pits, cold fires.

"There," Sieber said, "what's left of a hoop-and-pole game."

"They have children with them?" Clint asked.

"It isn't only children who play," Sieber said.

Mickey Free showed him a rock that was used to grind meal, and in another camp what was used as dance grounds.

"Are they running from us?" Clint asked, looking around the abandoned campsite.

"That depends on who you listen to," Sieber said. "General Crook thinks they're unaware of us."

"They'd be moving their campfires, anyway," Peaches said, "so that is no way to tell."

"They will have sentries posted every night," Sieber said. But the soldiers weren't traveling at night.

"So they do or don't know we're coming?" Clint asked.

"I think they do," Sieber said.

Suddenly they all became aware of A. Frank Randall, who was sort of staggering around the campsite, staring forlornly at items that would have made good subjects for photographs. Unfortunately, during the descent down an especially steep mountainside, the mules carrying all his camera equipment had misstepped and gone tumbling down the side of the mountain, camera equipment and all.

"Poor guy," Sieber said. "All he wanted to do was take photographs."

"He can still take notes," Clint said.

As if he heard Clint he suddenly took a small pad of paper from his pocket and began writing frantically.

"He'll have to draw his pictures with words," Clint said. "He'll become a better writer that way."

"Crook," Mickey Free said, and they turned to see the general walking toward them, with Captain Bourke just a little behind him and to his right.

"Mr. Sieber," Cook called out. "How long since they were last here?"

"Days, General," Sieber said, "maybe longer."

Crook turned to Sieber.

"Do you know other locations?"

"I do."

Crook slapped the palm of one hand with the gloves he held in the other.

"Let's hope we can find a fresher camp," Crook said. He turned to Bourke. "Get the men ready to move."

"Yes, sir."

"Mr. Sieber," he said, "get your scouts ready."

"Yes, sir, General."

Crook looked at Clint but said nothing. He turned and walked away, with Bourke right behind him.

"Probably figures he could have done without me up to now," Clint said.

"Is he paying you?" Sieber asked.

"You know," Clint said, "I never asked."

They moved on for several hours and then stopped to camp for the night. While they were camped some messengers came in just before dark and told of battle sites they had located.

Sieber was in with Crook while he received this information, and passed it on to Clint, Mickey Free, and Peaches around the fire later.

"Apparently, they found some sites where the Mexicans had encountered the Apaches. In one case it was obvious that the Apaches had ambushed the Mexicans, killed as many as they could."

"Shot?" Clint asked.

"Some of them," Sieber said, "but some had been killed with rocks."

"The Apaches may have rifles," Clint observed, "but they might be running out of ammunition."

"They'll steal more," Mickey Free said.

"They'll have to come out of the mountains to do it," Clint said.

"If we could keep them in the mountains until they run out . . ." Sieber said, and the others nodded. It was a sound suggestion, but easier said than put into action as a plan.

THIRTY

A scout came riding up and held a hurried conversation with Al Sieber. Sieber, in turn, told Clint and Crook what the man had said.

"They've located an inhabited camp," he said.

"How many hostiles?" Crook asked.

"There were about thirty."

"Were?" Crook asked. "The fools didn't engage them, did they?"

"Yes, sir, they did," Sieber said. "They attempted to surround the camp and were spotted. A battle took place, and most of the hostiles fled."

"Damn them!" Crook said. "All right, take us there. Let's see how much damage they've done!"

"Yes, sir."

Sieber told the scout to lead the way, and before long they were entering the camp, which was littered with slaughtered cattle and men. Apparently, the men of the camp had returned from a successful raid with many cattle, which they had proceeded to slaughter. There was butchered meat everywhere. And at this point they had engaged or been engaged—according to who was telling it—by the company of scouts.

The victorious scouts were in the act of plundering the

camp. They were loading their horses down with watches—both silver and gold—and American and Mexican money, all of which the Apaches had taken from Mexicans.

Two of the scouts came walking up to General Crook and the others, brandishing their captives, which numbered five children—three girls and two boys.

Sieber had inspected the camp on horseback and returned now to report to Crook.

"Wait," Crook said to the scouts who had the children. He looked at Sieber. "Go ahead, Mr. Sieber."

"Nine dead Apaches, sir. Traces of many others, but they must have been driven off."

"I see." He turned to Peaches. "Do you know any of these children?"

"Yes, I do," Peaches said. He pointed to one of the girls, who was almost full grown. She was very lovely with smooth skin and small breasts which, at the moment, were bare. She did not flinch beneath the hungry eyes of the soldiers and the scouts.

"She is Benito's daughter."

"Benito was with Chatto," Sieber said to Clint.

"Then this was Chatto's camp, not Geronimo's?"

"Most likely."

"What else did you get?" Crook asked the scouts.

"All the meat," one of them said.

"And many horses," another added. "And there is mescal, still cooking."

The two men looked pleased.

"Tsoe, will you take charge of these children? I'll want to talk to the older girl."

"I will do so."

Crook looked around and realized that the camp was ablaze, set afire by the scouts.

"Mr. Free?"

"Yes, sir?"

"None of these scouts are to have any mescal."

"Yes, sir."

"We can use some of the butchered meat. Have someone gather it up."

"Yes, sir."

"And confiscate any booty you might find," Crook said. "If we can't return it, it will go to the army, not to these scouts."

"Yes, sir."

The two scouts didn't understand. They thought that all of the loot they'd collected would be theirs.

"You men failed here," Crook said, "and failed miserably. You let most of the renegades get away, probably including Benito and Chatto. By now they've told Geronimo about us. This is no victory for you."

They looked crestfallen.

"Mr. Sieber?"

"Yes, sir?"

"I want the names of every scout who took part in this battle," Crook said. "They are to be paid off and sent on their way."

"Yes, sir."

"Idiots," Crook muttered.

THIRTY-ONE

"General?"

Crook looked up from his reverie. He had a cup of coffee in both hands and had been staring into it.

They'd camped a few miles from the site of the battle. Crook wasn't sure he wanted to abandon the location yet. They built several fires, made some coffee and beans, and most of the men avoided Crook, who was in a foul mood because of the day's activities.

Also around the fire were Clint, Mickey Free, and Sieber. It was Tsoe—"Peaches" was the name Clint thought of when he saw the man—who now appeared and spoke the general's name.

"What is it, Tsoe?"

"The girl," Tsoe said, "Benito's daughter, she says many of her people are ready to come back to the reservation."

"Is that a fact? Who?"

"She says Loco and Chihuahua would be glad to return. Also, many of the women and children."

"General?" Sieber said.

"Yes?"

"This may be a trick."

"What kind of trick?"

"Well, if we take on the women and children they'll slow us down, and Geronimo will be able to move more quickly."

"He's been moving quickly enough as it is, Mr. Sieber. Wouldn't you agree?"

"Yes, sir."

Crook looked at Clint.

"What do you think, Mr. Adams?"

"Why ask me, General?" Clint asked. "I have very little experience with Apaches."

"Yours would be a fresh viewpoint, sir, and as such most welcome."

Clint looked around and saw Tsoe, Mickey Free, and Sieber watching him.

"If any of the renegades want to come back I'd let them," Clint said. "You could always have some of the men take them back to the reservation. In fact, instead of letting go of the men responsible for the battle, let them take them back."

Crook stared at Clint, then looked at Sieber and Tsoe before speaking.

"Sound idea."

"Also," Clint said, warming to his subject now, "I think if any of them want to return it might affect the morale of the others. And if a *large* number of them were to return, so much the better."

Crook looked up at Tsoe and said, "Bring the girl here."

"Yes, sir."

Tsoe returned moments later with the girl. Someone had managed to find a garment that covered her breasts.

Crook spoke with her briefly through Mickey Free and she confirmed what Tsoe had said. She said most of the women wanted to return with the children, and that Loco and Chihuahua wanted to come back.

"What about Chatto? And Benito?"

"No," she said, "they do not want to return."

"You are Benito's daughter," Crook said. "Could you convince him to return?"

"I do not know," she said. "He listens to Geronimo."

"Ah!" Crook said, as if that explained it all. "Would you go to the people who want to return and bring them a message from me?"

She thought a moment, then said, "Yes, I will."

"Good," Crook said. He looked at Sieber. "We'll send her and one of the boys, as a show of good faith."

"Yes, sir."

Crook looked at the girl.

"What about you?" he asked. "Do you want to go back to the reservation?"

"Yes," she said without hesitation, "this life is too hard."

"You are no longer a captive, then," Crook said. "And neither are the other children." He looked at Tsoe. "See that they're fed. In the morning we'll let her and one of the boys go."

"Yes, sir."

Tsoe and the girl left, accompanied by Mickey, who seemed to have taken a liking to the girl. Crook reached for the coffeepot to pour another cup.

"Gentlemen?" he said, holding the pot.

Clint and Sieber were both surprised by the gesture, and held their cups out to be refilled.

"General," Clint asked, "how many women and children do you think there are?"

"I have no word of the size of that group," Crook said. "I know that Geronimo has been raiding with a party of thirty-five or thirty-six men. Chatto with slightly less than that."

"We'd better be prepared for five or fifty," Sieber said, "however many come in."

"Surely," Crook said, "it couldn't be more than fifty."

"I guess we'll have to wait and see," Sieber said.

"Gentlemen," Crook said, "I'm going to turn in. Tomorrow could be a big day for us."

"Good night, General," Sieber said.

"Good night," Clint added.

The general nodded to both of them and went to his bedroll. They did not bother erecting any tents, as the camp was very temporary and Crook had said it would be a waste of energy.

"What do you think?" Clint asked.

"Once they start coming in," Sieber said, "it's possible they won't stop until they've all come back."

"And Geronimo?"

"Like I said once before," Sieber said. "He's a reasonable man who can be talked to. Once he sees his people coming in, he might decide to join them."

"And Chatto?"

"I don't know about him," Sieber said. "He's young . . ."

"If Benito comes in, with Loco and Chihuahua," Clint said, "maybe that would do it."

"If it wasn't for what happened today," Sieber said, "we might have gotten them without firing a shot."

"I know what happened today was a mess," Clint said, "but maybe the incident will be what it takes to bring these people back in."

"You might be right." He wiped out his coffee cup and set it aside. "I think I'll turn in, too."

"I'm going to take a walk around camp," Clint said. "Just to stretch my legs before going to sleep."

"See you in the morning, then."

Clint nodded, stood up, and started taking a walk around camp.

THIRTY-TWO

Clint saw Mickey Free sitting next to Benito's daughter by a fire. He was talking and she was eating. By the light of the fire she was very lovely—and very young. Clint doubted that she was eighteen yet, and yet her body was almost that of a woman.

He continued to walk around the camp and saw Peaches talking to the captive Indian boys. Maybe he was trying to choose which one would go with the girl in the morning.

Scattered around the camp the men sat in clumps, and off in a corner sitting alone by a fire was Evan Watkins, the new corporal.

"Mr. Adams," he said, nodding.

"Corporal."

"Would you join me for a cup of coffee?"

"Thank you, I will."

The corporal poured it for him and they sat together. Clint thought that the invitation was a big step in the corporal's development.

"Why are you sitting here alone?" Clint asked.

"I still can't decide," Watkins said, "if I should be with them"—he indicated some privates sitting a few feet away—"or them," indicating some with extra stripes on their shirts, both corporals and sergeants.

"Are you going to let them make the final decision?" Clint asked.

"Oh, no," Watkins said, "I'll make the decision myself, it's just going to take a little more time."

"Well, take all the time you need," Clint said, "so you make the right decision."

"I will. Can you tell me something?"

"If I can."

"It's about tomorrow," Watkins said. "There's been some talk that some of the hostiles might be giving themselves up tomorrow."

"It's a possibility."

"Would that mean that we were near the end of this?" Watkins—and most of the white soldiers—had found the journey through the mountains arduous. The Indian scouts, on the other hand, went up and down the mountains like deer.

"That's another possibility," Clint said. "Some of them coming in might convince others to do the same."

"But what about Geronimo himself?"

"I'm told," Clint said, "that Geronimo is a reasonable man. This all remains to be seen, of course."

"Of course."

Clint finished his coffee and handed the cup back to Watkins.

"Thanks very much," he said. "I was just taking a walk around the camp before turning in."

"Uh . . . the Indian girl?" Watkins said quickly. "The, uh, pretty one?"

"Yes?"

"Is she going back to the reservation?"

"Eventually," Clint said. "But first she's taking a message to the others tomorrow to tell them they can come in and no harm will come to them."

"You mean the general's letting her go?"

"Her and one of the boys," Clint said, "but they'll be back."

"What if she doesn't come back?"

"I think she will," Clint said. "She sounded sincere to me."

"Well, maybe the general would like to send an escort with her, at least part of the way," the corporal said. "I could . . . volunteer."

Now Clint realized what was on the young soldier's mind. He was taken with the young Indian girl—but perhaps more sincerely so than the other soldiers, who had simply stared hungrily at her bare breasts.

"You know, that might be a good idea," Clint said. "If you were going to do that, though, you'd do well to make sure you get up nice and early to get to him with the suggestion. That means turning in—well, now."

"I'll do that," Watkins said. "Thank you, Mr. Adams."

"Sure," Clint said, "and good luck."

He walked away wondering if the young soldier had seen Mickey Free with the girl earlier.

Clint came upon one sullen group of scouts, and he realized that these were the men Crook intended to release, the ones who had fired on the camp and then looted it when the Apaches fled.

As he approached them he recognized only two of them, the two who had marched their captives over to Crook so proudly. They glared at him as if it had been his idea to berate them and fire them. He wondered if they'd been told yet that their jobs might have been saved—although he wondered how they'd feel about escorting women, children, and perhaps a few braves back to the San Bernardino reservation.

He walked past them without stopping and without meeting their eyes. They appeared to be in the mood to react belligerently if looked at the wrong way.

He arrived back at the fire he shared with Al Sieber and saw that the Chief of Scouts was wrapped in his blanket and snoring.

He wrapped himself in his blanket, closed his eyes, and sought the same condition.

THIRTY-THREE

Clint rose early the next morning and prepared a pot of coffee. Since Crook had slept closer to their fire than any of the others he got the first cup of coffee. Clint took the second.

When Sieber arose he nodded to Clint, greeted the general, and poured himself a cup of coffee.

"Mr. Sieber," Crook said, "when it's convenient I wonder if you'd fetch the Indian girl and one of the boys. We can get them started on their way."

"General," Clint said, thinking of Corporal Watkins, "it occurs to me you might want to have an escort take them part of the way."

Clint was hoping that Crook wouldn't ask why, because he didn't have an answer immediately handy.

"That sounds like a good idea, Mr. Adams. I'll assign a couple of men."

"Actually, sir, it wasn't my idea."

"Oh? Whose was it, then? Mr. Sieber's?"

"Not mine," Sieber said, with a shake of his head.

"No, sir," Clint said, "I was talking with one of your young corporals last night and he actually suggested it."

"Who was that?"

"Corporal Watkins?" Clint said. "Evan Watkins?"

"I don't know Corporal Watkins. Do you, Mr. Sieber?" Crook asked.

"Yes, sir," Sieber said. "Joined us the same time Clint did."

At that moment Captain Bourke came walking over to greet the general and, probably, to have a cup of coffee. He didn't get the chance.

"Captain, do you know Corporal . . ."

"Evan Watkins," Clint said.

"Watkins," Bourke said, frowning, "I believe I do, sir. He arrived at the same time Mr. Adams did."

"Would you find him and bring him to me, please?"

"Yes, sir . . . now?"

Crook looked up at the captain and said, "Right now, Captain."

"Yes, sir."

He looked at Clint and Al Sieber, as if wondering which of them had cost him his cup of coffee, then walked away.

Sieber finished his coffee and said, "I'll find Tsoe, and he and I can get the girl and one of the boys ready."

"I noticed him talking to the boys last night," Clint said. "Maybe he's picked one out already."

"Good," Sieber said, "I hope he has."

As Sieber walked away Crook said, "You seem to have been fairly active last night after I turned in, Mr. Adams. What else did you do?"

"Not much, sir," Clint said. "I did notice the group of scouts you were going to release huddled together. I wondered if they'd been told they might *not* be getting fired."

"I don't think they have," Crook said. He looked up and saw Mickey Free approaching. "Perhaps Mr. Free can take care of that for us."

"Take care of what, sir?"

Crook briefly explained what he wanted done, and Free agreed to go over and tell the men the news.

"What if they don't want to go back to the reservation, sir?" he asked.

"Then they can part company with us here and take their chances with Geronimo."

Free grinned.

"I think it's wise to give them those two choices, sir," he said, and walked off.

"Anything else we need to take care of this morning, Mr. Adams?" Crook asked.

"Well, sir," Clint said, "we might get somebody busy making something to eat."

"Capital idea," Crook said, "capital."

Clint wondered if he was going to come out of the Sierra Madre actually liking General George Crook.

THIRTY-FOUR

They had a breakfast of biscuits and bacon, and allowed the girl and the captive boys to eat. Tsoe had, indeed, chosen one of the boys to accompany the girl the night before, and Crook discussed the idea of an escort with Corporal Watkins, when Captain Bourke brought him to the general.

"I understand you and Mr. Adams discussed the idea of sending an escort with the Indian boy and girl we are sending out as messengers."

Watkins looked at Clint, who nodded once.

"Yes, sir."

"And it was your idea?"

"Yes, sir."

"Well, it's a good one, son," Crook said. "Now, perhaps you'd like to tell me who would make a good escort?"

"Well, sir," Watkins said, "I believe I would."

"Is that a fact?"

"Yes, sir."

"Corporal," Crook asked, "how many campaigns have you been on?"

"This is my first, sir."

"Mmm-hmm. And how many times have you been in these mountains?"

"This is my first, sir."

"I see."

Crook looked around and his eyes fell on Clint.

"Mr. Adams, would you consider accompanying Corporal Watkins to escort our messengers?"

"I would, General," Clint said, "but I don't know these mountains very well, either."

"That won't be a problem," Crook said. "Tsoe will also accompany you. The three of you will escort the messengers part of the way, and then return here. Is that understood?"

"Yes, sir," Corporal Watkins said.

"Understood, General," Clint said.

Tsoe simply nodded.

"All right," Crook said, "let's get them ready, then."

They didn't know exactly how far the Indian boy and girl would have to walk before encountering some of the renegades so they decided to give them a sack with some provisions.

Clint, Watkins, and Tsoe also took some provisions along for themselves, although Tsoe confided privately to Clint that he didn't think they would be away more than one night.

"There are several strongholds a day away from here," he said.

They saddled their horses. The girl, Benito's daughter, rode behind Corporal Watkins, and the boy rode with Tsoe. It was decided that if there was any shooting to be done Clint should be unencumbered during it.

They presented themselves mounted on the three horses to General Crook.

"You tell your people no harm will come to them," Crook instructed the girl through Mickey Free. "Tell them they will be fed, and then returned to the reservation. There will be no reprisals for the time they have spent in these mountains."

"No what?" the girl asked.

"No punishment," Clint said, and then Tsoe translated it more precisely into the girl's language.

"I understand," she said in English.

The boy who had been picked was the oldest boy, a couple of years younger than the girl, but a little taller than she was. He was very lean and his face seemed to be all angles and hollows. He did not understand English, and it was the girl who translated for him.

"All right, then," Crook said, "move out, and good luck."

Tsoe took the lead, with Watkins second and Clint third, and they left the camp that way, riding single file, which was the way they would spend most of their time.

THIRTY-FIVE

They traveled for half a day, occasionally dismounting to walk the horses up or down steep slopes or along a precipice. On occasion they found themselves in situations which would have been ideal for an ambush, but in each instance they came through safely.

Finally the girl said, "Stop here," and they did. Watkins lowered her to the ground and dismounted. The boy dropped nimbly to the ground, and Tsoe and Clint dismounted, as well.

"We should walk from here," she said.

Clint looked at Tsoe.

"There is a camp fairly near here," the Indian said. "It is probably better if they walk to it."

"Give them their supplies, then," Clint said. Watkins took the sack from his saddle and handed it to the boy, who peered inside curiously.

"Be careful," Watkins said to the girl, who looked at him oddly, then she and the boy began walking.

"We should camp," Tsoe said. "It will be dark soon. We can start back in the morning."

Clint and Watkins agreed, and the three of them went about making camp.

• • •

"She wouldn't tell me her name," Watkins complained, looking at Tsoe across the campfire. "Do you know it?"

"Yes."

"What is it?"

"That is not for me to tell you."

Watkins frowned and looked at Clint.

"Don't look at me," he said. "I don't know it."

Since neither man had any information for him, Watkins looked around. It was completely black all around them, and there was only the thinnest sliver of a moon above.

"We'll have to set watches," he said.

"I will take the first," Tsoe said.

Watkins looked at Tsoe, then at Clint. He obviously had something on his mind but didn't want to discuss it in front of the Indian.

"I don't have a problem with that," Clint said.

"I will sit away from the fire, in the dark," Tsoe said.

"Okay," Clint said. "Wake me for the second watch."

The Indian nodded and walked out into the darkness. As he was enveloped by it, Watkins moved closer to Clint and spoke in a whisper.

"Can we trust him?" he asked.

"To do what?"

"To stand watch," Watkins said. "Or will he just disappear on us? I mean, he's out in the dark. He could be anywhere."

"He's not going anywhere, Evan," Clint said.

"Well, who's to say he'll even warn us if the Apaches come after us tonight?"

"I think he will."

"You trust him, then?"

"I do, yes."

Watkins still didn't seem convinced.

"Well," he said, "I think I'll sleep with one eye open, anyway."

"That's up to you," Clint said, "but it'll make it that

much harder to keep watch when your turn comes. My advice is to get some sleep."

Clint rolled himself up in his blanket and lay down.

"Clint?"

"Yes, Evan?"

"Do you think she'll come back?"

"The girl? Yes, she'll come back."

"Why do you trust these people?"

"Evan," Clint said, "some of the most trustworthy people I've ever known have been Indians. Unlike white people, they do what they say they're going to do."

"And white people don't?"

"How did you get to be this age," Clint asked, "without paying attention?"

THIRTY-SIX

When Tsoe woke Clint he looked over at Watkins, who seemed to be fast asleep. Unlike Tsoe, Clint decided to sit by the fire. Since it had gotten pretty cold he didn't relish sitting out in the dark.

Clint wondered how much success Benito's daughter would have trying to convince her people to give themselves up and return to the reservation—the ones who didn't already want to, that is. To give themselves up they'd be making a conscious decision to turn away from Geronimo's leadership. It would be interesting then to see what Geronimo decided to do—and, for that matter, Chatto.

Clint poured himself a cup of coffee, realized it was the bottom of the pot, and made another one. The smell of coffee would certainly make no secret of their presence, if the fire wasn't already a dead giveaway.

He heard a sound behind him and turned quickly, but it was only Watkins.

"Can't sleep?" he asked.

"No," Watkins said, "and I smelled the fresh coffee."

"Sit and have a cup."

He handed Watkins a cup, then caught the young soldier looking at the fire.

"Don't look at the fire, Evan," he said.

139

"Why not?"

"It destroys your night vision," Clint said.

"Oh," Watkins said, then, "see . . ."

"See what?"

"I don't think I'm cut out to be a soldier, Clint."

"Why not?"

"I haven't been able to sleep since we got to the mountains."

"And what's the reason for that?"

Watkins hesitated, then said, "I'm scared."

"There's nothing wrong with that."

"There isn't?"

"No," Clint said. "In fact, being scared keeps you healthy, and alert."

"Yeah," Watkins said, "I'm so alert I can't sleep."

"That'll go away."

"When?"

"It might take a while," Clint said, "but it will. Trust me."

"I don't even know enough not to look into the fire," Watkins said. "If a band of Apaches attacked us now, what good would I be with no night vision?"

"You're too hard on yourself," Clint said. "Your vision will adjust in a few minutes, and then for the rest of the night you can just avoid looking into the fire."

"You make everything sound so easy," Watkins said.

"Evan," Clint said, "there's hardly anything about life that's easy—and it probably won't get any easier."

"Maybe I should just be a store clerk, like my father was."

"And was his life easy?"

"God, no."

"So what's the point? If you wanted to be a store clerk you could have stayed home—wherever home was."

"Pittsburgh."

"So you could have stayed in Pittsburgh, but instead you came west for some reason."

"To join the army."

"Which you did," Clint said, "and already you've earned a second stripe."

"You know how I got it?"

"How?"

"From a general who liked the way I cooked."

"You cook?"

Watkins nodded.

"Real well."

"Does Crook know that?"

"No," Watkins said, "and I don't want to tell him. I don't want to be a cook."

"Oh," Clint said. "Well, he won't hear it from me, then."

"This coffee is pretty good," Watkins said.

"It's the one thing I can make."

"Thanks for talking to me the way you do, Clint," Watkins said. "It really helps."

"I'm glad it does."

"But what am I gonna do when you leave? Who am I gonna talk to then?"

"You'll have to make friends, Evan," Clint said. "Friends who won't be scared off every time you get another stripe."

"I know it," Watkins said. "I've just never been very good at it. I've never been any good with people, not making friends, and not with . . . girls."

Clint sensed they were now going to talk about Benito's daughter.

"She's real pretty, isn't she?" Watkins asked.

"Yes, she is," Clint said, instead of pretending he didn't know who the young man was talking about. "She's also very young, and she's an Apache, Evan."

"I know," Watkins said, "I know both those things."

"To get yourself involved with an Apache girl would just make your life even more difficult."

"I know."

"Then why do it?"

"I don't know," the young soldier said with a shrug. "I just wanted to . . . to talk to her, but she wasn't very talkative."

"She's probably not very trusting of a white man in a soldier suit," Clint said. "Soldiers don't have a history of telling the truth to Indians—so you'd have that to fight, too."

"I know," Watkins said, "I'll just have to forget her."

"It wont be easy," Clint said, "but it's a sound idea."

Watkins nodded.

"Why don't you go and lie down for a few hours. I'll wake you in a while."

"Okay." Watkins stood up. "Thanks again, for everything, Clint."

"It's okay, Evan," Clint said. "It's all going to be okay. You'll see."

Watkins nodded again and went off to lie down.

Clint could tell that Watkins had finally fallen asleep, and he really wasn't tired, so he didn't wake the young soldier to take a turn on watch. He knew that was probably wrong, but he decided to let the man get some much needed sleep.

Consequently, he was still on watch when dawn came, and as the sun peeked up he thought he heard something out beyond the rocks. He listened intently, and then was sure he heard something. He woke Tsoe.

"What is it?" the Indian asked.

"Listen."

They both listened, and then Tsoe nodded.

"You have good ears," he said. "Indian ears. They are out there."

"The question is," Clint said, "are they going to stay out there, or are they going to come in?"

Tsoe shrugged and said, "You should wake him."

Clint went over to where Evan was sleeping and shook him awake.

"Wha—" The soldier started to sit up, wide-eyed, and Clint clamped his hand over his mouth and put his other hand against his chest.

"Take it easy," he said in a low voice. "They're out there."

Watkins nodded and when Clint removed his hand he asked, "Out where?"

"Beyond the rocks."

Watkins got to his knees.

"What do we do?"

Clint looked at Tsoe and said, "I suggest we wait and see what they're going to do."

"Yes," Tsoe said, "I agree. We will have some breakfast, and then if they have not made a move by then we will break camp."

"And then what?" Watkins asked.

"Evan," Clint said, "I think we're going to have to take this one step at a time."

Tsoe nodded and said, "You think like an Indian, too."

THIRTY-SEVEN

By the time they were ready to break camp the Apaches had not yet made a move.

"How many?" Clint asked Tsoe.

"Many more than we are."

"Could it be the ones who want to turn themselves in?" Watkins asked.

"Yes," Tsoe said, "it could be. Perhaps they are just going to follow us back."

"That sounds good to me," Clint said. "Better that than having it be a bunch of Chatto's boys."

They broke camp, saddled their horses, and prepared to ride out.

"We must stay very alert," Tsoe said.

"I can do that," Watkins said.

"And do not shoot unless I say so," the Indian continued. "Is this agreed?"

Watkins looked at Clint, who nodded.

"It's agreed, Peaches," he said. "You call the turn."

Tsoe nodded and said, "Then we must go."

They rode back to Crook's camp, always aware that someone was ahead of them, behind them, or above them in the rocks. All three of them were on the alert for the first shot, but it never came.

As they approached the camp they were challenged by a young private, who was rather jumpy.

"Hold it!" he said, pointing his rifle at Tsoe.

"Take it easy, Campbell," Watkins called out. "It's us."

"Corporal Watkins?"

"That's right," Watkins said. "Lower that rifle."

"Oh," Private Campbell said, "sorry, sir."

"Why so jumpy, soldier?" Clint asked.

"Somethin's goin' on, sir," Campbell said, "and we don't know what."

Clint said to Watkins and Tsoe, "Let's get to Crook."

"Let us by, Campbell," Watkins said.

"Yes, sir," Campbell said, moving aside. "Sorry."

"Forget it, soldier," Watkins said, and the three of them rode past.

"So you brought company back with you?" Crook asked when they finished their story. They were all in Crook's tent.

"It's possible, General," Clint said. "What about here?"

"We've had the feeling for some time that we're being watched," Crook said. When he said "we" he inclined his head toward Captain Bourke, who was standing off to one side, remaining silent.

"Have you seen anything?" Tsoe asked.

"No," Crook said, "nothing."

Tsoe nodded and said, "Then they are there."

"Who?" Bourke asked. "Who's there?"

Tsoe looked at Bourke.

"That is what we will have to wait to find out, Captain."

Bourke looked at Crook.

"Why wait, sir? Why wait for the savages to make the first move? I could take some men into the rocks—"

"We'd be lost in the rocks, Captain," Crook said, "and

they'd be at home. No, we'll do as Tsoe says and wait.''

"But, sir—''

"That's all, Captain. You're dismissed.''

Bourke wanted to argue, but in the end he just put his head down and bulled his way past the others to leave the tent.

"He's impatient," Crook said, "and I can't say I blame him. How did it go with the girl and the boy?''

"They're on their way," Watkins said, "sir.''

"More than likely they're there already, sir," Clint said. "If this is going to work, some of the Apaches should be coming in soon.''

"Maybe they even followed us here," Watkins added.

"Well, I'd prefer that you were followed by women and children and men who want to turn themselves in than by warriors who want to fight," Crook said.

"We outnumber them, don't we, sir?" Watkins asked.

"I'm sure we do, son," Crook said, "but they're up in the rocks and we're down here. Apaches say they're each worth ten white men—and up in those rocks, with rifles, they are.''

Crook got up and walked to the mouth of the tent.

"The men are jittery.''

"We know," Clint said. "We ran into one of them who almost shot Peaches.''

"I don't want them shooting at shadows," Crook said, "but they're close. Something's got to happen, and soon.'' He turned and looked at them. "If it doesn't, I'm going to have to make it happen.''

"How, sir?" Watkins asked.

"I don't know yet, son," the general replied, "I don't know yet.''

He turned, walked back to his field desk, and sat down heavily.

"You men can go and get some rest, and something to eat. You did a good job.''

"Thank you, sir," Watkins said, and they all three withdrew.

"How does he know we did a good job?" Watkins asked outside.

"Simple," Tsoe said. "We came back alive."

THIRTY-EIGHT

The first to appear were some women and children, carrying white flags of truce. They approached the camp and stopped when they saw the armed sentry. The soldiers on sentry duty had been instructed to admit any unarmed Apaches who approached the camp, and these were certainly unarmed.

The second batch were led by Benito's daughter and the boy who had gone with her.

By the time the third group arrived Crook and Bourke had designated an area for them to be taken to. Some of these were men, some old, some middle-aged, but no young warriors yet.

After that they came as if they were waiting in line, and it soon became obvious that there were more of them than had been expected.

"Still no warriors," Crook said, standing off to one side with Clint, Al Sieber, and Captain Bourke. "This many and still no real fighting men."

By the end of the day forty-five men, women, and children had come in, but none of the real fighting men. Crook sent for Benito's daughter.

• • •

"Chihuahua," she said, "wants to come in and is gathering his men."

Crook's mood immediately improved.

"When will he be here?"

"He hopes tomorrow," she said.

Crook looked around at the others in the tent: Clint, Al Sieber, Mickey Free, Tsoe, and Captain Bourke.

"If Chihuahua's band comes in maybe the others will follow."

"We're still in a wait-and-see situation," Sieber said.

"Yes," Crook said, "yes, we are, but it feels good now."

By the next afternoon the total number of Apaches who had surrendered was over a hundred—but still no real fighting men, no Chihuahua.

The Indian women tore flour sacks into pieces and tied them to poles, to indicate to the warriors that they were safe to come in. Still, none appeared.

"There are still men in the rocks," Tsoe said to Crook. "Watching us."

"Could it be . . . Geronimo?" Crook asked.

"It is possible."

"Maybe we should find out," Bourke said.

"How?" Sieber asked.

"Go up there and find out," Bourke said.

"Try it," Sieber said, "and you'll be shot to pieces."

"General—" Bourke started, but Crook cut him off.

"Mr. Sieber is right, Captain," he said.

"But—"

"We'll continue to wait."

And so they did.

That evening the men in the rocks showed themselves, and the women in the camp called up to them. Crook's men all came to the ready, should the Indians attack.

"No one fires," Crook said to Bourke and his other officers, "unless I say so."

"What are they saying?" Clint asked Mickey Free, as the women continued to call up to the warriors.

"They're telling them they don't want any fighting, and that they should come down."

"Will they listen?" Crook asked.

Sieber looked at him and said, "Wait and see, remember?"

"Do we know who is up there now?" Crook asked Tsoe.

"Yes," Tsoe said, "we know."

"Well . . . who is it?" Crook demanded.

Tsoe looked at them each in turn and said, "It is Geronimo."

THIRTY-NINE

Word spread through the camp that Geronimo and his men were in the rocks.

"There can't be more than thirty-five or -six of them," Bourke said, scoffing.

"They have the superior position, Captain," Al Sieber said.

"We have superior manpower, and firepower," Bourke said. He looked at Crook. "If we charge them we can overrun them and our casualties would be acceptable."

"But not minimal," Crook said.

"Sir," Bourke said, "we shouldn't just sit here and let them call the turn."

"Captain," Crook said, "I'd like you to collect volunteers to follow you up into the rocks to carry out your plan."

"Me?" Bourke said. "Uh, carry out the plan?"

"It's your idea, Captain," Crook said. "Who did you think would lead the charge?"

"Well, I, uh, thought, well—"

"Collect volunteers," Crook said, "and let me know how many you get."

"Uh, yes, sir."

As Bourke walked away Clint said, "You're not really

going to let that man lead a charge into those rocks, are you, General?''

''I don't think he'll get many volunteers to follow him up there, Mr. Adams,'' Crook said. ''Do you?''

Clint was liking General Crook more and more.

A few hours later two old men came down out of the rocks, messengers from Geronimo. They were brought to Crook by Tsoe, and Clint, Sieber, Mickey Free, and Captain Bourke stood by while they spoke.

''They say if they do not return, Geronimo will attack,'' Tsoe translated.

''Tell them not to fear, they will return. Ask them what message they bring.''

Tsoe conversed with the men in their own language, then turned to Crook.

''They say Geronimo wants to know what your intentions are.''

''Tell them my intentions are to take him and his people safely back to the reservation at San Bernardino. Tell them we mean no one any harm, but if we are attacked, we will fight, and we have many guns.''

Tsoe translated, then said to Crook, ''They say you have many guns, but you are in a bad position. They say they will tell Geronimo what your intentions are.''

''All right, then,'' Crook said. ''Let them go back.''

''General,'' Bourke said, ''why don't we keep one and send one back?''

''Why, Captain?'' Crook asked. ''What possible advantage could that give us?''

Bourke was obviously stuck for an answer.

''Send them back,'' Crook said to Tsoe, who removed the men from the tent.

''Captain,'' Crook asked, ''how many volunteers did you get for your plan?''

''Uh . . . none, sir.''

''Do you have any other suggestions?''

Bourke looked away.

"No, sir."

"Then you are dismissed, Captain."

"Yessir."

Bourke hastily left the tent.

"That man doesn't know the first thing about Indians," Crook said. "Mr. Sieber, how do you interpret Geronimo's sending those messengers down to us?"

"It's as I've said all along, General," Sieber said. "He's a reasonable man who can be talked to. This might be the first step toward a face-to-face meeting."

"I hope so," Crook said, "I sincerely hope so."

FORTY

Early the next morning Tsoe came to General Crook with a piece of information.

"What is it?" Crook asked over his first cup of coffee.

"Geronimo's sister, sir."

"What about her?"

"She's here in camp," Tsoe said. "She was one of the first ones to come in."

"A hostage, sir," Bourke said, but Crook ignored him.

"Will she go up and talk to him?" he asked Tsoe.

"Yes, sir."

"Sir," Bourke said, "if we let her go she can tell him exactly what the extent of our firepower is."

"Captain," Clint said, "don't you think Geronimo can see that from up there?"

"My thought exactly, Mr. Adams," Crook said. It was obvious that Crook felt he could depend more on Clint and on Sieber and the other scouts than he could on any of his officers—especially Captain Bourke.

"Let's send her up there, Tsoe," Crook said, "to emphasize what we told his messengers yesterday."

"Yes, sir."

"Do it now."

"Yes, sir."

Tsoe walked away and Crook looked at the other men, who had been waiting with him throughout this ordeal.

"What do you think?"

Sieber shrugged. "Maybe his sister can talk him into coming in."

Mickey Free nodded his agreement.

"I think he'll come in when he's ready," Clint said, "and it doesn't matter how many messengers he sends or you send."

"Why do you say that?" Crook asked.

"Well, at the moment he's dealing from a position of strength, isn't he?"

"Not technically speaking," Crook said.

"What do you mean?"

Crook looked around and didn't see Bourke lurking anywhere.

"Well, I hate to admit it, but Captain Bourke is right about one thing."

"And what's that?"

"We outnumber Geronimo," Crook said. "If we rushed him we'd suffer heavy casualties, but we *would* overrun him in the end."

"But we don't want to do that, right?" Clint asked.

"Not if we don't have to," Crook said, "no."

"Well," Al Sieber said, "let's see what the sister can do."

It was three hours later when Geronimo's sister came back down from the rocks. Tsoe walked out to meet her and walk her back into camp.

"Well?" Crook asked. "What happened?"

"She says Geronimo wants some of the scouts to go up and meet with him."

"That's fine," Crook said, "we'll send Mr. Sieber and—"

"No," Tsoe said, interrupting him.

"No?"

"Geronimo knows who he wants, and who he trusts."

"And who is that?"

"Dji-li-kine."

Crook frowned.

"Who is that?"

"His father-in-law."

Crook stared at Tsoe.

"Geronimo's father-in-law is one of our scouts?"

"Geronimo has been married six times," Tsoe said. "Dji-li-kine is the father of Zi-yeh."

"Is that all, then?" Crook asked.

"No," Tsoe said, "Chatto's brother-in-law is also here."

"Why wasn't I aware that we had family members of Geronimo with us?"

Tsoe shrugged. "You never asked."

Crook looked at Al Sieber.

"You're Chief of Scouts, did you know this?"

"I knew Dji-li-kine was with us, but I didn't know whether or not he was on good terms with Geronimo."

"Why didn't you think of using him as a messenger?" Crook asked.

"An in-law?" Sieber asked.

Crook, who was married, said, "Oh, yes." He looked at Tsoe. "All right, let's send them up."

"Yes, sir."

Once again Tsoe withdrew to arrange for someone to go up into the rocks.

Crook looked at Sieber.

"What do you know about this man, Dji-li-kine?"

"He's a white man by blood but was captured as a child by the White Mountain Apaches."

"And Geronimo married his daughter?"

"At some time, yeah."

"I didn't know Geronimo had been married six times," Crook said.

"It's considered a great honor to be married to him," Sieber said.

"I can imagine," Crook said.

Clint couldn't imagine being married once, let alone six times.

FORTY-ONE

When the messengers were ready Tsoe came and told Crook.

"Tell them to tell Geronimo that we want to give Chihuahua time to bring in the rest of his people. There will be no hostilities until then."

"I will tell them."

Tsoe relayed this message and then sent the two men into the rocks. Once again it was time to wait.

"The whites of my eyes must be brown, I've had so much coffee," Al Sieber said as he poured himself another cup.

Clint was looking up into the rocks.

"I wonder where he is," he said.

"Who?"

"Geronimo. I wonder which rock he's behind."

"I don't think it matters."

Clint shrugged.

"It's just something to do with the time."

"Why don't you take a walk around camp?" Sieber said.

"I would," Clint said, "but maybe those Apaches in the rocks would like to take shots at a moving target, just for practice."

"I doubt it," Sieber said, "not unless Geronimo himself took the first shot."

"Oh, fine," Clint said, "so then I'd have the honor of being killed by Geronimo."

"Hey," Mickey Free said with a grin, "if it's an honor to be married to him, just imagine what it's like being killed by him."

"Thank you," Clint said, "I think I will just sit right here and imagine it."

A couple of hours later the two messengers returned, and with them came three braves. Tsoe met them and walked them into camp.

"Chihuahua's men," he told Crook.

"Good," Crook said, "maybe now it will start."

And start it did. Over the next few hours men seemed to fall out of the rocks. They came walking in—Chihuahua's men—and surrendered their breech-loading Winchesters, their nickle-plated revolvers, or simply their bows and lances.

But the leaders still stayed out, and there were still enough men in the rocks to do some damage.

Crook called a meeting of the men he'd been using as a brain trust to date—Al Sieber, Mickey Free, Clint, Tsoe, and even Captain Bourke and a few of his lieutenants.

"We must do something to bring Geronimo in," he said. "When that happens most of the others will follow."

"How do you propose to do that?" Captain Bourke asked.

"By the simplest method possible," Crook said. "I'm going to let him capture me."

"What?" Bourke said.

"General," Sieber added, "that might not be the wisest course to take."

"Perhaps not," Crook said, "but I've got to get a face-to-face with Geronimo, and this seems the only way to do it—unless someone else has an idea?"

"Let me go," Sieber said.

"No," Crook said, shaking his head, "this is something I have to do."

"Then let me go with you," Sieber said.

"No," Crook said, shaking his head again, "I need you here."

"Well . . . someone has to go with you, General," Sieber said.

"Yes," Crook said, looking directly at Clint, "I agree."

FORTY-TWO

It was decided that Crook and Clint would venture out from the camp, supposedly to shoot game. In fact, they would shoot some birds, just to make it look good. General Crook felt sure that Geronimo would not miss the opportunity to grab him.

"How'd I get so lucky?" Clint asked Sieber, just moments before he was to leave camp with Crook.

"As it turns out," Sieber said, "the general likes you."

"Yeah, well, I was starting to like him, too, but that doesn't mean I want to risk my life with him."

"Relax," Sieber said, "at this point in the negotiations I don't think Geronimo will risk killing Crook."

"Fine," Clint said, "so he's safe. What about me?"

"Geronimo doesn't know who you are," Sieber said. "Maybe he'll want to find out."

"Yeah," Clint said, "maybe."

"Come on," Sieber said, "the general is ready."

Crook and Clint left the campsite on foot, both holding rifles. They walked until the camp was out of sight.

"I can feel them," Crook said.

"I can hear them," Clint said, "in the rocks."

"How?" Crook asked. "They're either barefoot or wearing moccasins. How can you hear them?"

"I just can."

"Well . . . we'd better shoot something," Crook said.

They both saw the bird at the same time. It was what most men called a "prairie chicken."

"Take your best shot," Clint said.

"You don't think I can hit it?"

"I wasn't challenging you."

"But you don't think I can hit it."

"Well, it is pretty far away."

"I'll have you know I was the top marksman in my class at West Point."

"General," Clint said, "that was a long time ago."

Crook looked directly at Clint.

"Do you want to bet?"

It seemed to Clint that the man had suddenly totally forgotten where they were.

"General—"

"Ten dollars."

"I don't think—"

"Twenty."

"All right," Clint said. "Okay, I accept your wager. Twenty dollars says you can't hit that bird."

"Accepted!"

Crook raised the rifle, sighted, and kicked up some rock chips just in front of the bird, frightening it away. Clint drew and fired in one fluid motion, realizing that they needed a dead bird if Geronimo was going to believe their reason for being out there.

"I don't believe it!" Crook said. "I couldn't hit it with a rifle, and you just drew and—"

"We needed a dead bird, General," Clint said.

"I know, but—I've never seen anything like that." Crook looked at Clint with renewed interest. "Are the stories about you actually true?"

Clint ejected the spent shell, inserted a live one, and holstered the gun.

"Let's go and get that bird," he said.

Clint walked ahead of Crook, who was still stunned by the swiftness and accuracy of Clint's shot. Finally, he roused himself enough to follow.

Clint reached the bird, bent down, picked it up, and looked at Crook—and beyond.

"What is it?" Crook asked.

"Behind you," Clint said.

Crook turned and saw half a dozen Indians, all armed with Winchesters. One of them stepped forward, fronted him, and said, "I am Geronimo."

FORTY-THREE

Geronimo said something to his men and they all moved forward. Clint and Crook were each disarmed by an Apache brave, and another took the dead bird from Clint.

"Why are you here?" Geronimo asked in English.

"We were hunting."

Geronimo pointed at Clint.

"He is not a hunter," the Apache leader said, "he is a killer."

"He is not a killer."

"His gun shoots straight, and swiftly," Geronimo said. "He is a killer."

"He came hunting with me because of his accuracy," Crook said.

"You are Crook?"

"I am."

"What is his name?" Geronimo asked.

"Don't speak around me as if I were not here," Clint said. "If the great Geronimo wants to know who I am, let him ask me."

Geronimo took his eyes from Crook and looked directly at Clint.

"What is your name?"

"Clint Adams."

There was no look of recognition in Geronimo's eyes, which were slate-gray. He stood tall and erect, the very picture of strength.

"Even the Apache have heard of the Gunsmith," he said, surprising Clint. He looked at Crook again. "You lied. He *is* a killer."

"I am no killer," Clint said.

"Stories of you have spread across this land—"

"Stories are not always true."

"I have seen you shoot."

"I shoot straight and swiftly," Clint said, "but I am not a killer."

"You have killed many men."

"Only those who tried to kill me."

"Why are you here?"

"I came at the request of Crook," Clint said. "He knows my reputation. He thought I could help persuade the great Geronimo to return with his people to the reservation."

"And kill me if I did not agree?"

"No."

Geronimo regarded both of them for a few moments, then said, "Come, we will talk."

He turned and Clint and Crook were herded by the others to follow.

They went to a small camp in the rocks and Geronimo, Chatto, Chihuahua, Clint, and Crook sat on the ground around a fire and talked.

"You did not come out to hunt," Geronimo said.

"No," Crook said.

"You let us capture you."

"Yes."

"Why?"

"So that we could speak."

"We should kill him now!" Chatto said.

He was younger than both Geronimo and Chihuahua, the perfect example of a fine young warrior. Tall, broad shoulders, solidly built, as if he'd been cut out of stone. He looked at both Crook and Clint with hatred.

"Be silent," Geronimo said, and Clint was surprised when the young warrior obeyed.

"You are letting Chihuahua's men surrender," Crook said. "What of yours? And Chatto's?"

"They are free to do as they wish," Geronimo said.

"They will not," Crook said. "They will act only when you do. You are their leader. You must come in first, and then they will." Crook looked around. "Chihuahua must come in, and Chatto—"

"I will not!" Chatto snapped.

"I said be silent!" Geronimo snapped. He lowered his voice when he spoke to Crook. "I must be sure that my people will be treated fairly and not punished for following me."

"They will be treated fairly," Crook assured him, "and no one will be punished. Not your people, and not you."

"This is true?" Geronimo asked Clint.

"It is what Crook promises."

Crook looked at Clint.

"What the Gunsmith says is true," Crook said finally. "I promise this, and I will keep my promise."

"What of the other white leaders?" Geronimo asked. "Will they keep Crook's promise?"

Crook hesitated. Clint had spoken truthfully, he could do no less.

"I will try to make sure that they do," Crook said, "but can Geronimo promise that Chihuahua and Chatto, and other of your leaders, will not try to escape?"

It was Geronimo's turn to hesitate now, and then he said, "I cannot promise for them."

"And I cannot promise for the other white leaders," Crook said, "only for myself."

"Crook's word is good," Geronimo said. "He is a great leader."

"And so is Geronimo."

"Geronimo is not a great leader if he makes us surrender," Chatto said vehemently.

"Silence—"

"I will not be silent," Chatto said. "My men and I will not surrender."

"You should follow Geronimo," Clint said. "He is a wise and experienced leader."

"I am a wise leader," Chatto said, pounding his fist against his chest.

"You are young," Clint said, "and headstrong. You will lead your people to disaster."

Chatto got to his feet quickly and Clint uncrossed his legs, looking up at the young warrior.

"You say Crook and Geronimo are great leaders?" he demanded.

"Yes."

Chatto looked at Geronimo.

"I will follow you if you decide to surrender . . ." he said.

"That is good."

". . . but only if he defeats me."

He pointed at Clint.

"What?" Clint said.

"You must fight for what you believe," Chatto said. "If you can defeat me hand to hand, I will follow Geronimo *and* Crook."

"And if I can't defeat you?"

"Then I will never surrender," Chatto said, "and you will die!"

FORTY-FOUR

Clint was given time to consider Chatto's proposal.

"What do you think?" Crook asked.

"I think I should have never come to San Bernardino," Clint said. "Do you see the size of this man? And he's younger than I am."

"Twenty years, at least."

"Well, fifteen, maybe."

"I think you have to fight him."

"I think you don't want to pay me the twenty dollars you owe me."

Crook took out a twenty-dollar gold piece and said, "Here."

"Thanks."

"Now you have to fight him."

Clint frowned. "Double or nothing," he said finally.

"What?" Crook said.

"Double or nothing," Clint repeated. "If I fight him and win I get another twenty dollars."

"And if you lose?"

"You can take this twenty dollars off my dead body."

"You can't lose," Crook said. "If you do, Chatto and his men will stay out here and continue their raids."

"You'll have to stop him, won't you?"

"Not me."

"What?"

"I told the president I would come here and take Geronimo back to the reservation. I've done that. Whether you win or lose he's going to come back with me. He can send someone else out to fight Chatto. Maybe he's got himself another Custer somewhere."

"Oh, sure," Clint said, "that's all any of us needs is another Custer."

"Well, then, you have to win, don't you?"

Clint took a deep breath and let it out disgustedly.

"Let's get this over with."

"Who gets to choose the weapons?" Crook asked Geronimo.

"The Gunsmith was challenged," Geronimo said. "He chooses."

"Hand-to-hand," Clint said.

"The white man is afraid to fight me with a knife," Chatto said with a wicked grin. "It does not matter. I will kill him with my bare hands."

Geronimo had his men form a circle around Clint and Chatto. He and Crook also stood as part of the circle.

"Fight!" Geronimo said.

Chatto roared and charged Clint, who sidestepped and stuck his foot out. Chatto tripped over it and went sprawling. Clint leapt on his back, got one arm in a hammerlock he learned from a wrestler, and slid his other forearm beneath Chatto's chin to cut off his wind. The younger man strained and struggled, but he could gain no balance. His own aggressiveness had been his undoing, and Clint had been able to immediately capitalize on Chatto's first mistake.

He leaned over and spoke into Chatto's ear.

"Do you see? You are younger, faster, and stronger than I am and yet you are helpless because of my experience."

Chatto could not reply, because he could not breathe. His

face was getting redder and redder, and Clint knew that if he kept the hold on much longer he'd kill him.

He released his hold, stood up, and stepped back, waiting to see what Chatto would do.

The young warrior got slowly to his feet, one hand to his throat as he coughed and gasped, trying to get his breath back. He turned and faced Clint, a murderous look in his eyes, but he did not charge again.

"Our fight was to be to the death."

"I chose not to kill you."

"I would have killed you."

"I know it."

"You are a fool."

"Maybe."

"The fight is over," Geronimo announced. The braves who had formed the circle groaned in disappointment.

"If we were to fight again," Clint said to Chatto, loud enough for all to hear, "you would defeat me. I have no doubt. Today, my experience allowed me to defeat you, but it would not happen again."

Chatto rose to his full height and looked at the other braves, who looked away. Clint, by his admission, had saved face for the Apache warrior.

Chatto looked at Geronimo and said, "If you go back to the reservation, we will follow you."

"Good," Geronimo said. He turned and looked at Crook. "We will go back."

FORTY-FIVE

Clint rolled over in his bed and stared down at Ginny's back. She'd been so glad to see him again that she immediately took the rest of the day off and practically dragged him back to his hotel. He had a different room this time, but the bed was about the same, and it groaned and complained as they made love, straining against each other, clawing at each other. Her passion was such that in trying to match it—and succeeding—Clint had nearly collapsed the bed.

Now he stared at the lovely line that traveled down the center of her back and disappeared between the cheeks of her ass. He ran his finger down, then leaned over and traced it with his tongue. When he got to her butt he kissed her there, then gently bit each cheek until she awakened.

"Now that I'm awake," she said, "and you're down there, what are you gonna do?"

"Make sure you stay awake."

He slid one hand beneath her belly, palm up, then slid it back down until he was cupping her, the hairy wiring against his palm. He rubbed his middle finger along her slit until she moistened and then he slid his finger inside. She lifted her hips and moaned, and soon—as he continued to stroke her—she rose to her knees.

"Come on, come on . . ." she implored him.

He got to his knees behind her, grasped her hips, slid his thickened penis up between her smooth thighs, and then slipped into her easily, and fully. . . .

When Clint and Crook had come down from the rocks with Geronimo, Chatto, Chihuahua, and some of their men the others had stared in disbelief. Quickly an area was cordoned off to accommodate the surrendering warriors. They were relieved of their weapons, which piled up in a tent off to one side.

"What happened out there, General?" Bourke asked. "We heard shots."

"We were shooting at birds," Crook said.

"Birds?"

"That's right."

"Why?"

"It was a bet," Crook said. "I lost twenty dollars to Mr. Adams."

"Forty," Clint said.

Crook looked at him and then allowed himself a smile.

"That's right, forty." He took another twenty-dollar piece from his pocket and handed it to Clint, who accepted it. After all, a bet was a bet.

By the next morning there were 220 "hostiles" in camp, and they all had to be fed. This was putting a serious strain on Crook's supplies.

Geronimo had breakfast with Crook, along with Chatto, Chihuahua, Benito, Clint, Al Sieber, and Mickey Free.

"What's going on between you and Chatto?" Sieber asked at one point.

"What do you mean?"

"He keeps looking over at you," Sieber said. "One minute he looks like he wants to kill you, the next minute like he respects you."

"I think," Clint said, "it's a little of both."

• • • •

The trip back to the San Bernardino reservation was slow because many of the Indians were on foot. They finally reached it, though, and Clint was able to take his leave of General Crook's force.

"I'll accompany Geronimo to the reservation," Crook said to Clint.

"Is this where he'll stay?"

"I don't know," Crook said. "Here, San Bruno, Fort Apache, who can say? I just said I'd bring him in. I have no say in where they place him."

"Do you think he'll stay this time?" Clint asked.

"Frankly?"

"Yes."

"Until his people are being mistreated again," Crook said.

"You know that's going to happen?"

"I'm afraid it will," Crook said. "There are always people—profiteers—who are looking to profit by the misery of others. The supplies that are meant for the Apaches will offer a great temptation to some people."

"I understand."

"Perhaps if he bolts again," Crook said, "I'll be called on to bring him back again."

"You won't be able to make the same promises to him," Clint said.

"I'll have to think of others, then," Crook said.

"Why?"

Crook shrugged.

"It's my job."

He extended his hand.

"Thank you for your help."

"Thank you for the forty dollars."

Crook laughed and said, "I hope it was worth it."

As the soldier rode away, Clint laughed and said, "It wasn't."

• • •

"Are you leaving today?" Ginny asked him as he got dressed.

"Tomorrow morning," he said.

"Then we'll have tonight?"

He laughed.

"If I survive it."

"You will," she said, "but I don't know if I will. I can't feel my legs."

He laughed and kissed her.

"Where are you going now?"

"To say good-bye to a friend," he said, and left the room.

Clint found Al Sieber in the saloon, at the same table where he'd been sitting when Sieber had found him that first time.

He got himself a beer and joined the scout at the table.

"I wondered when you'd show up," Sieber said.

"I had another friend who needed attention."

"I thought someone was missing," Sieber said, looking around. "Can't say I blame you. Come to say good-bye?"

"Yep," Clint said. "When are you leaving?"

"In a little while. Crook's got some job for me."

"Already? No rest."

"Why should I rest? You did all the work."

"Did he tell you what happened up there?"

"He did."

"I got lucky."

"So I heard," Sieber said. "It sounds like you also did the right thing for Chatto."

"I didn't want to fight him again."

Sieber laughed.

"Can't say I blame you for that." He reached into his pocket and came out with a folded envelope. "I've got something for you." He put it on the table between them.

"What is it?"

"Wages."

"For what?"

"General Crook asked me to deliver this and tell you that he didn't think forty dollars covered it, either."

Clint touched the envelope, then took his hand away.

"Don't you want to see how much it is?"

"No."

"You're not gonna take it?"

"No."

"Why not?"

"Because I'm not sure I did the right thing by helping you get Geronimo back to the reservation."

"If he didn't go back," Sieber said, "eventually he would have ended up dead."

"Maybe," Clint said, "that would have been better for him. What's he got to look forward to now? Getting old on the reservation? Dying an old man?"

"Maybe."

"That's not the way a great leader should end up."

"Why did you help, then?"

"It was the right thing to do, at the time—or so I thought."

"So what am I supposed to do with this money?"

"Bring it back to Crook," Clint said. "Tell him I want to donate it to the Apaches on the reservation. Tell him to use it to get them some supplies—and to make sure they get them."

"Okay, if you say so."

Sieber picked up the envelope and put it back in his pocket.

They each finished off their beers and Sieber said, "Walk me out?"

"Sure."

Clint had seen Sieber's pony tied up outside. When they reached it Sieber put out his hand.

"Whether you think you did the right thing or not," he said, "thanks."

"Sure," Clint said. "I won't say 'anytime,' though, if you don't mind."

"I don't. What are you gonna do now? Leave?"

"In the morning," Clint said.

"What about now?"

Clint grinned and said, "Now I've got to go back to the hotel. I've got some more good-byes to say."

Watch for

THE LADY KILLERS

198th novel in the exciting GUNSMITH series
from Jove

Coming in July!

J. R. ROBERTS

THE GUNSMITH